DOCTOR DON'T LEAVE
DISHY DOC SERIES. BOOK THREE

PARKER DEE

INTRODUCTION

Parker Dee is the pen name for Carol Rivers. Sunday Times best-selling author

FOREWORD

If you would like to receive Carol's news and updates on all her romance series, please sign up for her newsletter at the end of this story.

CHAPTER 1

'THERE'S NOT a tooth in this one's head,' sighed Betty Atkins as she bounced her baby son on her knee. 'Not like the rest of the kids at twelve months.'

Alissa smiled at the healthy but toothless baby. 'Give Sam another couple of months and he'll probably have a full set. There'll be no stopping him then.'

Betty Atkins laughed. 'Well, he'd better get a move on if he wants a pecking order in this family. With another one on the way, it'll be every man for himself at the breakfast table.' She patted the gentle slope of her stomach. 'This is the last one - definitely!'

'How's Jamie?' Alissa wondered if Betty's nonchalance covered real anxieties about her marriage to Jamie.

'Oh, same as usual.' Her patient shrugged. 'He's off like greased lightning in the mornings and I hardly see him the rest of the day. Barely have time to cook him his breakfast let alone help on the farm.' She paused, biting down on her lip. 'I s'pose we'll cope. We always seem to.'

Alissa glanced at the three Atkins children, standing behind their mother. Mark was seven, Emily nine and Donna four years of age. Sam had been only six months old when Betty had conceived again.

Alissa was amazed that Betty still managed to get up at five o'clock every morning let alone cook Jamie breakfast.

The Atkinses had been farmers for generations and Betty Atkins was a typical farmer's wife, bursting with rosy good looks, but the dark smudges under her eyes revealed the strain the family had been under ever since Emily had been diagnosed as being autistic. Jamie had distanced himself since then, pleading pressure of work, leaving Betty to cope with all the domestic problems.

'Betty, have you thought about - ?' Alissa began, then stopped, deciding not to broach the subject of family planning whilst the children were present. But Betty had read her GP's mind.

'Jamie says it'll have to be me that has the operation,' Betty said resignedly. 'You know what men are. And farmers are even more adamant in that respect, something to do with carrying on the name...says farmers are an endangered species, would you believe?'

Alissa wondered why Jamie Atkins seemed to ignore the pressure his young wife was under. As a farmer, he might be a member of an endangered species, but Betty was running a close second. Moreover, Emily would have to have special attention soon if her autism was to be dealt with properly.

'Anyway, back to Sam here.' Alissa tickled the baby's chin. 'No teeth yet, but nothing to worry about. In all other departments he's fine. Is there anything else you'd like to talk about while you're here?' Alissa glanced at Emily who gazed into space while her brother and sister giggled between themselves.

Betty shrugged, catching the direction of Alissa's glance. 'Em's about the same, I suppose, except the tantrums seem a bit worse. And she's having problems at school - I just wish I had more time to spend with her.' Just then Emily roused. She jerked awkwardly into her brother and, startled, he retaliated by pushing her back. Emily toppled onto four-year-old Donna and immediately there was a bitter squabble.

'Stop it you lot,' shouted Betty ineffectually, hoisting Sam onto her hip and standing up. 'Better go before they turn your surgery into a zoo,' she added wearily, rolling her eyes at Alissa.

'Bring them to the clinic on Friday.' Alissa rose and, smiling at the children, opened the door. 'We can have a better chat while they play in the creche.'

'If I can get away,' Betty muttered, herding her noisy children into the corridor. 'Jamie's busy ploughing up a field on Friday. I'll have to be around for the milking.'

'You aren't still working in the dairy?' Alissa asked in surprise.

'Only to supervise Jason,' Betty answered hurriedly, not meeting Alissa's eyes. 'At sixteen he's still a bit green, but at least he does all the heavy work.' Alissa knew that the Atkinses had taken on help and she had hoped Jamie would accompany his wife to surgery for their overdue chat regarding family planning, but Betty's response today revealed that there was little chance of that.

'Betty - ' Alissa began, but the young woman was already chasing after her brood, eager to avoid any difficult questions.

Alissa sighed as she watched them go. Poor Betty. She really needed a break. Was Jamie Atkins blind to his wife's exhaustion? Alissa wondered.

A few minutes later Alissa followed the Atkins family into Reception. As she entered the large, white-walled room with its low oak beams and decorative inglenook fireplace, the hum of conversation was punctuated by the resonant one o'clock chime of the Minster.

Alissa cast her eyes over the room. Who, if anyone, remained to be seen? The two girls behind the desk, Ruth Mathews and Lyn Hall, were busy on the computers. Three young mums who had attended the toddlers' clinic sat on the chairs, still chatting.

Above the hum of voices Alissa heard a crash. One of the toddlers had pulled over the small table on which the magazines were kept.'Monty!' cried one of the mothers. 'I told you to leave the magazines alone, naughty boy.'

But Monty seized his opportunity to wreak havoc. He turned his attention to the low shelf on which the children's books were kept, and swept several onto the floor. His mother leapt from her seat but he nimbly escaped her grasp. Alissa darted forward and scooped him into her arms.

Instead of screaming, the little boy sneezed and everyone cried, 'Bless you, Monty!'

'It's the dust from the paper.' Monty's mother laughed. 'It always makes him sneeze.'

'Me, too,' said Alissa as a shower of dust motes surrounded her wavy blonde hair. 'I think I'd better give him back to you before I - '

Monty landed safely back in his mother's arms just as Alissa sneezed. She slipped a tissue from her pocket, wagging her finger at the irrepressible toddler. 'You've started me off now, Monty!'

'Once a wish, so the saying goes,' said a deep voice behind her. Alissa turned to find Max Darvill grinning under his shock of raven black hair.

Alissa smiled mischievously. 'A month's holiday in the Caribbean wouldn't go amiss.'

'Don't you dare!' Max Darvill threatened. 'I couldn't lose you now.' As though he realised what he had said, he added swiftly - though not quite in time to hide his embarrassment, 'Bearing in mind our full schedule for the next few weeks.'

Alissa felt an unexpected twinge of disappointment. What had she thought he meant, for heaven's sake? That he didn't want to lose her in a personal sense? Ridiculous, she told herself, feeling a flush creep over her cheeks at the very thought.

She had to admit, though, in different circumstances her wish might have been to know Max a little better. In the four months or so of their new partnership she had discovered very little about him.

Not that he hadn't always been polite and courteous. Since Christmas and the official opening of the Minster Practice, all their energies had been spent on the transfer of the archives of the old surgeries to the new one. That had been a mammoth task in itself.

However, once completed, the popularity of their new location, formed from two separate practices, had taken everyone by surprise. The backdrop of medieval minster and market-place was - as Max had suggested a year ago - ideal for a surgery. The section of L-shaped cottages which had once been used as a craft centre needed only minor changes. All had been completed by Christmas and together with Max's young partner, Erin Brooks, and Alissa's colleague, Alec Rogers, they had celebrated the opening in January.

Alissa had not had cause to regret the merger. Sometimes she felt a little guilty that her peaceful life with Sasha had been disrupted but, then, as Sasha was full time at school now, life was easier all round. The irony was that six-year-old Sasha and eight-year-old Bas Darvill, Max's younger son, attended the same school and had become firm friends, and Sasha tended to find out more about Max's life than she did!

'Bas is going to stay with his mummy,' Sasha had told her one day as they'd walked the short distance to school. 'She's got a new boyfriend called Claude. Why haven't you got a boyfriend, Mummy?'

'Because there is no one I love as much as Daddy,' Alissa had answered, squeezing Sasha's hand tightly. She'd known it was important to reassure her daughter whenever she had the opportunity.

'But Daddy won't come back, will he? He'll stay in heaven with the angels, won't he?'

'Yes, darling,' Alissa had agreed, relieved in one sense that Sasha had accepted Mike's death as she had, but saddened that she could never make up for his loss.

'Bas's mummy and daddy are still alive on earth.' Sasha had frowned. 'Why don't they live together any more?'

'That happens to some mummies and daddies,' Alissa had tried to explain, realising that now Sasha was at school there would be more questions like this.

'If I had a daddy,' Sasha had answered, 'I would want him to stay with us for ever.'

Alissa's heart had constricted. 'When you're a little bit older,' she had added gently, 'you'll understand.'

Alissa found herself staring into a pair of questioning grey eyes. She blinked, refocusing on reality.

'And so is your daughter going on the trip by any chance?' Max was asking.

'Oh, the visit to Shermore Manor Park?' Alissa guessed, wondering how much of Max's conversation she'd missed. 'Sasha's rather young.' She hesitated. 'I did wonder if she'd appreciate it.'

'Hmm,' murmured Max. 'That thought had struck me, too.'

'The school is asking for volunteers among the parents,' she added, glancing at Max as they walked into the corridor. 'Perhaps I'd better wish for a fairy godmother to go on our behalves.'

Max grinned, revealing an unexpected flash of white teeth. 'Yes, that might be a good idea.' He was suddenly serious, as a thought seemed to strike him. 'Perhaps we should get together and - '

At that point raised voices in Reception made him stop. Turning back, he narrowed his eyes. 'I didn't think we had anyone left to see today, did you?'

'Not as far as I know...'

'Better take a look, I suppose.' He placed his hands on her shoulder in a polite gesture to move past her, but the sensation of his fingers on her silk blouse made her jump. Alissa held her breath, letting it out slowly as he walked away. He had never touched her before and for a moment she was shaken. Gaining control of herself, she was relieved that he seemed not to have noticed and, listening to the growing clamour in the waiting room, she followed him.

'If you'll just take a seat for a moment, Mrs Haigh,' Ruth Mathews was saying as she stood behind the reception desk.

'But can't you see my son is ill?' a blonde woman in an expensive - looking white trouser suit said stridently. Alissa recognised her immediately as Max's ex-wife, Priscilla Haigh.

'Yes,' agreed Ruth, glancing down and smiling at the small boy by her side, who was obviously having trouble breathing. 'I must just check that Dr Darvill is free to see you - '

'Of course he's free to see his own son!' Priscilla Haigh retorted.

'Whatever is going on, Priss?' Max strode forward, his eyes going down to Bas's distraught face.

'It's his asthma,' Priscilla sighed, pushing Bas forward. 'He was perfectly fine one minute, then this ... just when we were to catch the plane. Of course there was no way we could fly so I drove straight back down here.'

'Had he used his medication?' Max knelt in front of Bas, cupping his white face gently in his hands.

'Of course he had. Or at least I think so. Have you, Bas?'

Bas nodded, a tear sliding down his cheek. 'I must be in Paris for this evening,' his mother went on, examining her watch with a worried frown. 'I just don't know what to do.'

But Max wasn't listening. He took the boy's hand and without a word strode past both Priss and Alissa. Priss hurried after them and Alissa watched her hurry down the corridor into Max's consulting room.

Ruth Mathews shrugged as Alissa walked towards the desk. 'Poor little mite. He was trying so hard not to cry.'

Lyn nodded. 'I suppose that means Dr Darvill won't want to see anyone during the lunch-hour.'

Alissa frowned. 'Well, if there are any emergencies, I'll see them.'

'But it's your half-day,' Ruth protested worriedly. 'You're supposed to be off duty now.'

Alissa shrugged. 'Astrid is with Sasha until half past two so I've another hour or so to spare.'

The girls nodded and said no more, although Alissa guessed what they were thinking. Priscilla had appeared at the surgery twice before and each time she'd managed to upset someone or other. The last time it had been a patient who had objected, quite rightly, to being asked to wait whilst Max's attention - and equilibrium - were disturbed.

On her way back to her room, Alissa felt a twinge of pity for Max. But why did he tolerate such behaviour? she asked herself. The only conclusion she could draw was that, despite their divorce and Priss's remarriage, which had ended in disaster, they must still be close.

Alissa shuddered. The unpleasant scene had brought back memories of her own unhappy past. She knew all too well how it felt to have to deal with a difficult partner. In six years of marriage to her late husband, Dr Mike Leigh, most of her illusions and all of her dreams had been shattered. Given that Priss was still very much a part of Max's life, wouldn't it be natural to assume that they still spent time together?

CHAPTER 2

BACK IN HER room Alissa sat at her desk and lowered her chin into her hands. It wasn't often she thought about Mike, at least not while she was at work. Being busy, that was an effective panacea but at home it was more difficult, especially at night. Though she had loved Mike deeply, her life had once been as turbulent as Max's. Once her existence felt as though it were balanced on the side of a volcano. Now at least each day she could wake up without that sense of foreboding.

Alissa took up her pen and began signing the prescriptions in front of her. Priss Haigh certainly had a knack of disturbing the peace, and it looked as if she was about to do so again. However, as sympathetic as Alissa felt towards Max, Priss was his problem, not hers.

At two o'clock she would leave and go home. After that, Max would have to cope on his own.

It was five minutes to two when a firm knock caused Alissa to look up from her work. Max opened the door and poked his head around. 'Have you a moment, Alissa?' Strain was evident on his features.

'Of course. Come in.'

He entered and sat down in the chair beside her desk. Alissa was relieved to see that Priss did not follow him in. 'Sorry about the interruption,' he apologised. 'Ruth said that you waited specially.'

Alissa nodded. 'I thought I should in case we had an emergency of some sort. I was just about to leave, actually.'

'Oh, I see.' He looked worried.

'How is Bas?'

'Better now, thanks, but unfortunately I find myself in a bit of a fix. I wonder if I might ask a favour?'

He had never asked for her help before - indeed, as far as she knew, he had never asked anyone for help. He was a deeply private person and she knew he would not, under normal circumstances, ask a favour. 'How may I help?' she asked at once.

'Priss had a prior engagement and had to fly to France,' he explained in a tight voice. 'Bas was meant to be going with her for the half-term holiday. But, as you saw, he had a bad asthma attack and we thought it wiser for him to remain at home.'

'And you have a full surgery,' Alissa prompted, guessing what might be coming next.

He nodded, trapping his lip under his white teeth, obviously finding the conversation an effort. 'Aaron, my elder son, is away camping until tonight, otherwise he would have kept an eye on Bas. Mrs Dunphy, my housekeeper, is on holiday. However, Bas can rest here in the staffroom for a bit - until I'm finished. I wonder if you could possibly take over a few of my patients so that I can leave earlier?'

'Would it be an idea,' she suggested on impulse, 'if I took Bas home with me? I'm not doing anything special this afternoon. Sasha will be delighted to see him. Then you could take your surgery without worrying about Bas.'

He looked startled and she smiled. 'I've had a little medical experience so you won't need to worry about Bas's asthma.'

Relief washed over his face. 'But this is supposed to be your half-day, Alissa.'

'I don't mind.'

'Well, if you're sure? I still feel it's an imposition to expect you to look after Bas for the whole afternoon.' Alissa smiled. 'Not at all. I'll get my things.'

She rose and collected her bag. They stood for a moment by the door. Once again he seemed uncertain.

'This really is very good of you,' he said quietly.

'What are ... doctors for?' She had been about to say 'friends for' then had changed it. She laughed, hoping to hide her sudden blush. Their relationship had never edged past professionalism in all the time they'd been working together. It would hardly have been accurate to term it as friendship.

Rather awkwardly he smiled. 'Well, let's see how Bas is doing,' he said. Pausing briefly to open the door, he waited for her to walk past him.

In Max's room, Bas was still lying on the bench, his face white, but his breathing was more relaxed. On the trolley lay the nebuliser, an instrument powered by electricity, used to filter a fine spray of dissolved drug into a patient's mouth. Bas must have been quite poorly, she realised, for Max to have deemed it necessary.

Max helped his young son to sit up. Affectionately he smoothed back the boy's rumpled dark hair.

'I feel a bit better,' Bas croaked.

'Well done,' Max said gently.

'Has Mum gone?' Bas asked as he lowered his feet to the ground.

Max nodded. 'She'll ring you at home this evening.'

Bas looked at his father. 'Mum said she's going to take me and Aaron to Disney in the summer holidays. I hope I don't have my asthma then. Couldn't we go on a boat instead of a plane?'

'I don't see why not,' Max said quietly. 'I'll talk it over with Mum at a later date. Meanwhile, we've got to get you sorted out today. I have a surgery until five but Dr Leigh has kindly suggested you go home with her and spend the afternoon with Sasha.'

Bas's large grey eyes - a replica of Max's - widened until they looked like mini-moons. 'You mean, go to Sasha's house *now*?'

Alissa smiled. 'Sasha will be pleased to see you, I'm sure.'

Bas remained silent and for a moment Alissa wondered if he might not want to go with her. It would be natural for him to be anxious after his attack and he had just recovered from the disappointment of his abandoned holiday.

'Sasha's desperate to have some help with her new laptop. Any chance you could offer a few suggestions?'

Bas, at once enthusiastic, nodded.

Alissa glanced at Max. There was an expression in his eyes that made her heart still for a few moments before she collected her thoughts. 'Well, then,' she said, taking a breath, 'that's all settled.'

Bas slid down off the bench and Max, still looking uncertain, swept Bas's school blazer and cap from the chair. 'I carry a spare set of clothes in the back of the Land Rover for the boys,' he told Alissa as they all walked into the corridor. 'I'll give them to you before you go.'

'Fine.' Alissa smiled, her heart racing a little as once again she met his gaze. She couldn't think why she was reacting like this - all she was doing was helping someone in a fix!

Dr Erin Brooks glanced from her window, absently curling a lock of thick chestnut hair around her index finger.

She sipped at the coffee Ruth Mathews had made her, a poor replacement for her missed lunch-hour but the sacrifice had been worth it. She had just returned from the dressmaker's and the final fitting of her wedding gown. The bodice of the beautiful dress in white satin had only to be decorated with tiny white rosebuds before it was finished. Erin's bubbling excitement over her wedding in July reflected in her lovely green eyes.

For a moment she was tempted to phone Simon at his City stockbroker's office in London and share the good news. But, knowing Simon, he would make all the right noises, oblivious to her comments. As always, his attention would be riveted to the computer screen in front of him.

Carefully putting her excitement to one side, Erin's thoughts went to her first patient, eight-year-old Hannah Brent. Two weeks ago Hannah had displayed symptoms of a food allergy. The little girl had been sick after eating strawberries and had developed a troublesome rash.

Erin was concerned. This year she had diagnosed more allergy cases than ever before. Was it something to do with the rural environment? she wondered. At the next practice meeting, she decided, she would raise the issue. The practice nurse, Mo Green, had privately suggested forming an allergy clinic - an idea Erin was beginning to warm to.

It wasn't the sight of Max Darvill in his dark suit, striding towards the Land Rover Discovery, that brought Erin out of her preoccupation over Hannah, but the two figures accompanying him. Alissa, hand in hand with Bas, waited for Max to unlock the vehicle. Max pulled out a rucksack and handed it to Alissa.

Erin sighed reflectively. She liked both Max and Alissa a great deal. In a sense it had been Max who had made it possible for her to achieve her dreams of country life. His patience throughout her training year had given her much - needed confidence and when - unexpectedly - he had offered her a permanent post at the old surgery, she had accepted without hesitation.

Not that Simon had been enthusiastic about the idea! Moving from the City to a sleepy Dorset market town had hardly been his idea of heaven. But finally he had agreed. Her happiness had been complete - a traditional minster wedding, a secure and fulfilling career at the Minster's popular new practice and a gorgeous, seventeenth-century cottage to call home.

Erin's attention, at risk of straying again, was finally drawn back to the little group in the car park. Alissa opened the rear door of her car and Bas scrambled in as Max watched.

Now there was a couple who really suited one another ...

Max was tall and handsome - albeit in a rather remote way. At thirty-eight he had never married again after his divorce. Erin thought of Priscilla Haigh and wondered if she would ever allow Max to make a future for himself. Going on events of the past few years, it was unlikely, she thought.

Alissa was all that Priss was not - sympathetic, easy to talk to and sincere. Despite the tragedy of losing her husband at such a young age, she never indulged in self-pity - unlike Priss, whose main preoccupation was herself and her troubles.

And at thirty-three Alissa was still stunningly attractive, Erin thought admiringly. Slender and petite, she always looked elegant. The pale ivory linen suit she wore today hugged her dainty figure and complemented her halo of short, wavy blonde hair. Yes, were Priss Haigh to disappear from the scene, Alissa would make the perfect partner for ...

Erin sighed again. Priss vanishing, that was highly unlikely. With two divorces behind her, Priss had come full circle back to the one person who always seemed to be there for her.

Erin felt a sudden rush of gratitude for her own good fortune. A challenging career and a beautiful home in the country with a wonderful man like Simon - all her dreams had come true.

By the look of it, Erin thought interestedly as she peered through her window, Alissa was getting to know Max a little better. They had always kept a distance between them, which Erin found rather curious. She sensed there was definite chemistry there and watching them now - well, perhaps she was right after all.

Erin drew away from the window and returned to her desk. The way would not be made easy for romance. Priss might not want Max while she had other distractions to occupy her, but their duration was notoriously short-lived. Then, bored and disillusioned, she always returned to haunt Max.

CHAPTER 3

BAS AND SASHA occupied themselves in the study for the best part of the afternoon on the computer. Alissa asked Astrid, her Swedish au pair, to supervise the children until she was able to do so herself. Bearing in mind Bas's asthma, she gave Astrid instructions to watch over them until she had prepared tea. However, Bas was untroubled by his breathing and at four o'clock Alissa fed them, relieved to discover that Bas had a healthy appetite and was none the worse for wear.

After tea the children asked to play in the summerhouse. Alissa decided she would do some gardening, at the same time keeping an eye on them.

She gave Astrid the rest of the afternoon off, then changed into shorts and a cotton sun-top. She found a spot near the summer-house and settled down by one of the borders to weed.

She loved their home of two years, relieved to have sold the cumbersome old Victorian house after Mike's death. It had held no happy memories - just painful ones which she preferred to forget. So, opting for a large, conservative modern house with mellow brick-work and turned gables over dormer windows, she had chosen Green Gables.

The house move had allowed both Sasha and herself to start afresh, and one of the things Alissa had indulged herself in was growing flowers. It was in the garden that she could lose herself completely. She was lost in thought, unaware that a shadow had fallen across her as her thoughts were, yet again, in the past.

'It's a beautiful garden,' a familiar voice said, and Alissa swivelled around, shading her eyes from the sun.

'Max - I didn't hear you!' She stood up, self-consciously brushing the crumbs of earth from her shorts. 'What time is it?'

He shrugged apologetically. 'It's after six, I'm afraid. I'm sorry I'm late, but we had a late surge of activity at the surgery.'

'I hardly noticed,' Alissa replied easily. 'The children are playing in the summer-house. Bas hasn't been troubled by his asthma. I'm happy to say.'

He smiled. 'Well, thank you again.'

'Would you like a cup of tea or a cold drink?' She felt it might seem rude not to invite him in.

'Something cool,' he agreed at once, 'would be great.'

'I'll just tell the children you're here.' She turned and walked to the summer-house where the children were absorbed in a game. Explaining that Max had arrived, she told them to come to the kitchen as soon as they had finished.

When she returned to Max, he smiled at her and drew a white handkerchief from his pocket, dabbing gently at her cheek. He tipped up her chin as he did so, turning her face to the light. 'There, that's better. Just a sprinkling of soil.' He grinned, 'I'll avoid the freckles, they're much too pretty to disturb.'

For a moment there was an awkward silence as his hands dropped away. Resisting the urge to smooth her fingers over the tingling area of skin he had just touched, Alissa smiled hesitantly then turned back along the path.

He walked beside her, suddenly stopping at the overflowing borders of flowers. 'They're breathtaking,' he told her. 'How do you do it? I shouldn't imagine you get very much time for this, do you?'

'An hour or two after Sasha is in bed and Astrid, our au pair, has gone to her language class. The garden is quiet then, a pleasant time to be working in it.'

'I wish I could say the same for our wilderness,' he remarked wryly, transferring his gaze to the prolific vine that spilled blue flowers above the kitchen door. 'I'm afraid I haven't your creativity. Aaron will mow the lawn occasionally, but he flatly refuses to be persuaded into what he calls green-wellie-land.'

Alissa laughed. 'How old is Aaron?'

'Fourteen, fifteen in a couple of weeks.'

'Obviously he's got his exams - ' Alissa began, but Max grimaced.

'I rather think exams come way down the list at the moment. I regret to say it's the opposite sex that seems to occupy Aaron's mind ... one young lady in particular.'

'Most fifteen-year-old boys have girlfriends, don't they?' Alissa shrugged. 'We only have to listen to our patients to know that.'

They paused at the kitchen door and Max looked down at his feet. 'Yes, that's true. What worries me is that I don't feel quite so objective about my own son as I do my patients' children. Aaron has gone camping with a mixed group of friends. I suppose it's safe enough but, you know, you always worry.'

'I'm sure Aaron is a sensible young man,' Alissa said, nevertheless wondering how she would react when it came to Sasha's turn to claim her independence.

Max stepped into the kitchen after her. 'This is a lovely room.' He gazed around admiringly. The arched window shed light across the terracotta floor tiles and a fan of sunlight spread over the white worktops. Light was reflected everywhere and spilled off the pale green walls. As he studied the room, Alissa noticed how broad his shoulders were as they strained against the crisp blue cotton of his shirt. His one concession to the heat was that his shirt-sleeves had been rolled up over his tanned forearms. She found herself wondering if the silky spirals of black hair that wove their way under the material continued their passage over the rest of his body. She checked herself sharply. It must be the heat, she thought as a waft of lemony aftershave trickled under her nose and a shiver went over her skin.

'I'll find the children,' she said and was about to hurry into the hall when he stopped her.

'Before you go, Alissa. About Saturday's trip ...'

She frowned. 'The school outing?'

He nodded. 'I'm not on duty this weekend, so I thought - '

'You would offer your services as a fairy godmother?' she teased, and they both laughed.

'Something of the sort,' he admitted.

'You've really decided to volunteer for the school trip?'

'Not exactly.' He hesitated. 'I phoned the school this afternoon and because of a lack of support at the last minute they've cancelled it.'

Alissa frowned. 'Oh, dear, that makes me feel rather guilty. Sasha is going to be disappointed.'

He nodded. 'Me, too, but to make up for it, well, the thought occurred to me that I might take Bas anyway. I wondered if you'd be interested in joining us?' When she didn't reply he added hurriedly, 'It's the least I can do after today.'

At that moment Bas and Sasha came running into the kitchen. Overhearing the last part of the conversation, Sasha asked excitedly, 'Are we really going with Bas to the animal park on Saturday?'

Alissa hesitated. 'Well ...'

'Please, can we, Mummy?' Sasha pleaded. 'My friend Lucy says that Shermore Manor has some seals there, too, and they're my favourites.'

Max chuckled, arching a dark eyebrow. 'I'm afraid I've started something now.'

'Please?' begged Sasha, her dark plaits bobbing up and down on her green T-shirt. 'We'll be really good ...' She turned to Bas and tugged at his sleeve. 'Won't we, Bas?'

Bas blushed and looked at his father under his lashes.

'Of course,' Max said with a shrug, 'if you are already doing something else ...'

'We aren't, are we, Mummy?' Sasha squeaked, and Alissa was forced to agree with her daughter that they had nothing planned for the weekend.

Max smiled. 'So, that's settled. An early morning start and we're off to Shermore Manor. Shall we take the Discovery? Let's say nine-thirty. That should give us a head start before the traffic builds up.'

Sasha jumped up and down. 'Thank you, Mummy! Thank you, Dr Darvill.'

Max laughed. 'My pleasure, Sasha. I'm grateful to you for entertaining Bas today.'

As the children ran into the garden, Alissa pushed back a lock of wavy blonde hair and looked up at Max. 'You really don't have to do this, you know. Bas was no trouble at all.'

'Let's just say I'm overdue for some quality time with Bas,' he responded casually. 'Having your company and Sasha's will make the experience even more enjoyable.'

Alissa didn't know how to respond as he looked into her eyes and held her gaze. Finally she looked away and walked to the door, wondering if she had been wise to agree for Sasha's sake. But there was no changing her mind now, she realised as she discovered the two children talking excitedly about which animals they were most looking forward to seeing.

'Bye,' Bas called to Sasha. 'See you on Saturday.'

Max smiled and waved goodbye. Alissa and Sasha watched them climb into the Discovery.

'I like Dr Darvill,' Sasha said as she stood waving to Bas. 'He's nice.'

Alissa watched the vehicle disappear. It had been difficult to refuse Sasha lately. Because of the pressures at work, she had found herself giving in to requests. Small things, like an extra half-hour's reading time before bed, but it was enough to increase Sasha's confidence in widening the boundaries. Alissa hoped that this arrangement was not going to be added to the list; she hadn't really had time to think Max's offer through. Perhaps he had only suggested the combined outing because the school would have phoned her to cancel the trip. Knowing Max, he would have thought it impolite not to have made the offer.

A practice meeting was scheduled for half past five the next day. Though Alissa had passed Max in the corridor that morning, they had spoken only briefly and no mention had been made of the Saturday excursion. As Alissa took her place beside Erin Brooks in the staffroom, she decided to put the matter out of her mind for the time being. The evening was too beautiful to spend fretting. Soft, balmy air trickled in through the open windows of the staffroom and summer scents filled the half-timbered room. Alissa sat back in her chair, allowing herself the luxury of watching Max who was talking to Alec Rogers.

He sat to her far right, his head bent over his notes. Suddenly he looked straight at her, as though he'd felt her eyes on him. Quickly, she looked away.

'Everyone here?' said Alec, frowning around the room. 'Yes, fine. So we'll begin, shall we?' After a few moments the hum of conversation died. 'We've several things to discuss. Erin has suggested the formation of an allergy clinic for the duration of the summer. And Alissa would like to discuss Emily Atkins who, as we all know, is autistic. As each of us sees the Atkins family from time to time, I think we should decide together on how we can best help the family.'

Alissa was relieved that Emily's case was on the agenda. She wanted to ask for support in her application to the local authority to fund Emily's place at a special school for children with learning difficulties. Betty needed help swiftly and the official departments were dragging their feet.

During the pause Erin leaned across and whispered, 'I heard about Priss Haigh yesterday.'

Alissa nodded, aware of her friend's perceptive gaze. 'Bas had an asthma attack at the airport.'

'Where's his mother now?'

'She had to fly back to Paris that night.'

'And she just *left* him?'

Alissa shrugged. 'He certainly wasn't fit enough to travel and Max had a full surgery. It seemed the obvious thing to do to offer to take him back home with me.'

Erin raised her eyebrows. 'It's not often Max asks for anyone's help.'

Alissa decided to change the subject. 'Have you told Simon your dress is almost finished?' Alissa lowered her voice as Mo Green, the practice nurse, aired her concerns about allergy problems.

'No, I'm leaving it until the weekend,' Erin whispered back. 'Simon's taking me out to dinner and staying until Sunday evening.'

Alissa saw how happy her friend was. She hoped things would work out well for Erin, though by all accounts Simon Forester, her fiancé, lived life in the fast lane. Would he adjust to country life? she wondered. Well, if the look on. Erin's face was anything to go by, Erin had her future securely mapped out. She loved country life and was a good doctor. And from what Erin had told her, Simon had agreed to leave the hustle and bustle of the City behind him.

Alissa listened to Erin giving her views on the subject of a new allergy clinic. She wondered if Erin had talked Simon into the idea of buying a property yet. Despite the fact that Simon had pressed for a modern town house on one of the new developments, Erin had her heart set on a seventeenth-century cottage. With a sharp pang, Alissa remembered how exciting buying her first house with Mike had been. In those days she had been so in love she would have agreed to live in a garret if Mike had suggested it. But, instead, Mike had bought into the busy seaside practice on the Kent coast ...

'Alissa?' Erin was nudging her. 'It's your turn to speak.' 'Oh - yes, thanks.' Alissa picked up the document that lay on her lap, a prospectus for the school she hoped Emily might be able to attend. She glanced around the assembled faces and, pushing the shadows of the past to the back of her mind, began to speak. She gave brief details of the special centre for autistic children; Betty Atkins required written testimonials from the doctors and any nursing staff who were familiar with Emily's case.

'I'll write a report if you like.' Annie Partridge, the health visitor, spoke up. 'I know the family quite well.' Alissa nodded. 'Thank you, Annie, a report would be helpful.' She turned to Alec Rogers. 'You're familiar with the family, Alec?'

The senior partner nodded. 'I've known Jamie and his parents as long as I've lived in Hayford Minster. They're a hard-working farming family. Jamie was actually a very gifted child - far brighter than his brother and two sisters. But his parents couldn't afford to give him the education he needed. They expected him to work on the land and after his father died, leaving the farm in his hands, that's exactly what he did.'

Alissa frowned. 'So Jamie was a gifted child?'

'Oh, yes,' Alec went on. 'Jamie had a very high IQ. It's a great pity he drifted, but thirty years ago the facilities for these kinds of children were scarce.'

Alissa wondered why neither Betty nor Jamie had ever mentioned this. Might it help to explain why Jamie Atkins seemed to expect so much of his family yet paid scant attention to their needs?

'Well, to recap,' Alissa continued, 'Emily didn't start to speak until she was almost three years old, after being diagnosed as autistic. She finds interaction with people difficult, almost impossible, and she's given to tantrums. Betty tells me she repeatedly asks questions but never responds to the answers. Her reading and writing is poor, her co-ordination weak. The result is serious behavioural problems, and since neither Betty nor Jamie have time to give her more attention I can foresee the problem becoming worse. I feel that a special centre would meet all her needs.'

There was a general murmur of agreement. Alissa was relieved that everyone seemed sympathetic. But then Max looked up, a frown spreading across his forehead. 'Are we talking of Emily leaving home permanently for a residential place at the school?' he asked abruptly.

'It's possible, yes.' Alissa was bewildered by his tone. 'Have you any objections to that, Max?'

He paused, then nodded slowly. 'As a matter of fact, I have. I don't believe taking Emily out of her environment will resolve her fundamental problems within the family.'

'But she's obviously at risk -' began Alissa.

'Her education is somewhat lacking, yes,' interrupted Max sharply, and the room fell silent. 'But do we know how Jamie feels about this? What are his views on Emily's future?'

'Jamie Atkins refuses to come in to discuss Emily,' Alissa explained. 'He appears to leave all the decisions to Betty.'

Max paused. 'My reaction is to err on the side of caution. Not rush into campaigning for Emily when we don't really know the full facts.'

Alissa tensed. 'I'm hardly rushing, Max. Emily is nine. She may well be ten by the time she is accepted for a place.'

'All of which doesn't necessarily mean that Emily should be removed from her surroundings,' he pointed out swiftly.

Surprised by his hostile attitude, Alissa felt the eyes of everyone at the meeting focused on her. 'My point,' she continued uneasily, 'is that Emily's circumstances have not improved since she was diagnosed as autistic. In fact, they've worsened.'

Max nodded. 'Yes, I am aware of that.'

Erin bent forward and whispered, 'Emily was Max's patient at the old surgery.'

Alissa bit her lip. She had been unaware of that. In fact, she knew hardly anything about Jamie's or Betty's history, her main concern being Emily. Alissa looked across the room at Max. His grey eyes met hers in a long stare and she cleared her throat. 'In that case, perhaps we can review the situation with both Jamie and Betty Atkins present? Shall we raise this again at the next practice meeting?'

Alec Rogers nodded. 'Good idea. I think we're all in agreement that we are concerned for Emily, indeed the whole family.'

Alissa smiled gratefully, then dropped her head to look at her notes. But she wasn't reading them. Why had Max not mentioned his views before? Why make it look as though she was blundering into something she knew nothing about?

Alissa pushed Emily's notes back into a folder and sat upright. Max was no longer looking at her. His face was turned towards Alec who was addressing the meeting again.

'Don't take it to heart,' Erin said softly beside her. 'Max is a professional all the way down the line. He doesn't mean to be abrupt. Betty Atkins and her family are a bit of a vexed question, I think.'

'Do you know why?' Alissa asked.

Erin shook her head. 'Not really. The problems began when I first came to Hayford Minster during my training year. Betty booked in with me instead of Max. He never said why she avoided seeing him and nor did she.'

'And you saw Betty regularly after that?'

'No. I think she thought I was too inexperienced to deal with her problems.'

Alissa frowned. 'Her notes say very little in a personal vein. Most of the details relate to the children. When she first came to me in January the case seemed straightforward enough.'

Alissa was, nevertheless, upset by Max's remarks. It was Betty herself who had pressed for the special school place for Emily. And, as far as Alissa could see, with good reason.

Together with Erin, Alissa rose and left the meeting. By the time she arrived home that evening, she had almost decided to cancel Saturday's outing. The uneasy feeling persisted that to mix her personal life with her professional one was unwise. But cancelling now would seem childish. There was nothing for it, she decided, but to go as arranged.

As it was, when Saturday morning finally arrived, Sasha was so full of beans that Alissa forgot her doubts. She couldn't help but join in with her daughter's excitement.

'Shall I put on my new shorts?' Sasha asked at the breakfast table as Alissa prepared a picnic. 'The ones with the polar bears on?'

Alissa wondered what she herself should wear. 'Yes, and I'll take jeans and sweaters for us, too, in case the weather changes.'

'As it's almost my birthday,' said Sasha, spooning the last of her cornflakes hurriedly into her mouth, 'can I wear my new T-shirt, too?'

Alissa turned from the picnic hamper and smiled. 'I don't see why not.'

Alissa had taken Sasha shopping during half-term. It had been the only available time before Sasha's birthday in June. The T-shirt and shorts had been Sasha's choice. Alissa glanced at the uneaten toast on the table. 'Darling, finish your breakfast before you dress.'

Sasha pushed her bowl and the remainder of her breakfast away. 'I'm too excited to eat any more.'

'Well, drink your fruit juice, then. I don't know what time we'll arrive at Shermore. We might have to wait a while before the picnic.'

Sasha scraped back her chair, her cheeks pink with excitement. 'Bas says we'll get to Shermore by eleven o'clock. He's been there before.'

'Has he?' Alissa frowned. 'Dr Darvill made no mention of that.'

Sasha shrugged. 'Bas was only a baby. He says he doesn't remember any of the animals.'

Thoughtfully, Alissa slid the packed sandwiches in the hamper. 'Well, at least it will be a nice surprise for both of you.'

Sasha skipped off to her bedroom and Alissa paused in what she was doing. She wondered if Max and Priss had visited Shermore Manor together. It was quite a popular place - she had often considered taking Sasha, but had decided to wait until Sasha was old enough to appreciate the outing. Alissa closed the lid of the hamper. She had prepared roast chicken and cranberry sandwiches, hard-boiled eggs and savoury snacks. Idly, she reflected that Priss hardly seemed the sort to wander around an animal park and that a health farm seemed more appropriate to her taste.

Upstairs in her bedroom a few minutes later, Alissa opened her wardrobe and took out several pairs of cotton trousers. None of them appealed, neither did shorts. They would be appropriate for the day but somehow they didn't seem quite right.

On impulse she took out a dress. It was a pretty cotton frock in a soft blue swirling material, the exact shade of her eyes. With her blonde hair and eyebrows bleached by the sun and the light tan she had gathered while gardening, the dress really did seem perfect.

Ten minutes later she stood at the long pine mirror, frowning critically at her reflection. Did she look overdressed? What would Max wear? Then she realised she wanted to look her best - and that was only natural, wasn't it? After all, a girl had her pride - pride which had been seriously damaged from her brush with Max at the practice meeting!

It was, as Bas had told Sasha, half past eleven by the time they reached Shermore Manor. Max had driven steadily along country roads, avoiding the motorway. Alissa sat quietly beside him, watching the countryside unfold. The two children were sitting in the back of the Discovery, making enough conversation for all of them put together.

At the big iron gates of the park the queues began. Cars snaked back onto the main road, causing congestion, and tempers flared as several cars broke down in the heat and had to be pushed onto the grass verge.

'Drat,' muttered Max as they were forced to wait. 'I had hoped to avoid this.'

'Is it always so popular?' Alissa asked. She added quickly as he looked at her, 'I understand from Sasha that this isn't your first visit.'

Max looked back at the road. 'Yes, that's right. Aaron was about eight at the time, Bas two.' He didn't enlarge on the topic and Alissa made no further comment, guessing that the visit must have been made with the boys' mother.

'Can't we just leave the Discovery outside in the lane and walk in?' called Bas from the rear seat.

'No, I'm afraid not,' answered Max firmly. 'There are car parks inside the grounds. Just be patient. It won't be long now.'

'Which animals are we going to see first?' Bas wanted to know as the minutes ticked by.

'Donkeys,' giggled Sasha mischievously. 'Everyone likes donkeys. We've got one in the field behind our house, haven't we. Mummy? They make a dreadful noise that wakes us up in the mornings.'

'Like this?' Bas pinched his nose and hooted.

Max and Alissa, glancing at one another, began to laugh.

'I like seals.' Sasha giggled. 'I'm going to swim with the seals when I grow up.'

'You mean you're going to swim with the dolphins,' Bas said knowledgeably.

'No,' answered Sasha firmly, 'cos dolphins only swim. They can't sit on rocks, like seals do, and clap their fins.' Their amusement continued as the queue shortened and Max eventually drove through the gates and towards the turreted manor house. By the time they'd parked and found the animal section, the children were tense with excitement.

As Sasha had guessed, there were donkeys and horses, too, elegant shires with their decorative harnesses and thick manes. Farm Corner had everyone gasping at a newly born litter of piglets, and an aquatic section housed beautifully coloured tropical fish.

The seals were, as Sasha had also foretold, clapping their fins, anticipating lunch. At the side of the beautiful blue pool, designed for audience participation, their keepers threw in fish for the seals to swallow. Bas pointed to a young pup followed by four of his brothers who basked at the water's edge. The children admired them from the perimeter fence, absorbed in their antics.

'Enjoying it?' Max asked Alissa, his grey eyes moving over her face.

Alissa nodded as he leaned on the wall beside her. 'Yes, very much.'

'I wanted to talk to you before we left,' Max said hesitantly, his eyes seeming to bore into her face. 'I had the feeling you were offended by what I said at the practice meeting.'

Reluctant to spoil the happy atmosphere, Alissa shrugged. 'I was a little upset, yes.'

He looked down at his clasped hands. 'I would have preferred to have talked to you about the Atkinses in private,' he said quietly. 'Unfortunately your suggestion took me by surprise.'

'But isn't it obvious that Betty needs help with Emily?' Alissa questioned. 'What else, as a doctor, can I do but help with Betty's request?'

There was a brief silence before he looked up. 'The Atkinses' history is a complicated one - '

'A history which doesn't appear to be part of their notes,' Alissa interrupted quickly, wishing they hadn't touched on a subject which could spoil the day.

'Yes, that's true,' he admitted. He paused again, finally thrusting a hand through his hair. 'The point is, I simply felt it was unfair to be judgemental.'

Alissa turned to face him. 'Of whom?'

Before he could reply the children came racing over to them, bored now that the pups had disappeared beneath the surface of the water.

'We're hungry,' Sasha informed them, her brown ponytail swinging over her shoulders. 'Can we eat our picnic now?'

Alissa turned to Max. 'Perhaps we'd better find a spot before it becomes too crowded.'

'Yes, of course.' His grey eyes met hers fleetingly. 'Over there perhaps, in the shade of the trees.'

Although Alissa was relieved that the subject of the Atkins family had been dropped, she was, nevertheless, still curious to know what he had meant by his last remark.

'Come on, Sash,' Bas called. 'We'll find a place.' Sasha, following in Bas's footsteps, hurtled off towards the wooded area designated for picnics.

'Well, at least lunch has been settled democratically enough,' Max said in a wry tone. He paused, arching a dark eyebrow. 'We'll finish our conversation later - meanwhile, why don't you follow the children while I fetch the picnic?'

She agreed, allowing her gaze to linger on him as he walked away. She watched his dark head, clearly visible above others in the crowd, slowly disappear into the distance. He was dressed in light-coloured chinos and a denim shirt, and the easy swing of his broad shoulders held her gaze until he was finally out of sight. It was odd, she thought, how different he seemed once away from the surgery. Today in the car his dark hair had flopped over his forehead and his lopsided smile had made her wonder how it would have felt to reach up and smooth that hair back into place. Turning to follow the children, she wondered again, as she had many times during the day, if Shermore Manor had brought back memories for him. However, if there had been thoughts that disturbed him, he had shown no outward sign. She was suddenly grateful that, as busy Kent doctors, she and Mike had spent so little time together, even less time after Sasha was born. Had she visited a place as beautiful as this with Mike and Sasha, she would have avoided it now at all costs. The pain of recollection would have been too hard to bear.

CHAPTER 4

THEY ATE the picnic under the shade of the trees and, once rested, returned to the animal park eager to sample the pony rides. After a trip on the train that encircled the park they made their last stop the guided tour of the manor house. A climb of the fifteenth-century tower around which the manor had been built left them breathless. It was cool and pleasant inside the elegant rooms, but the children were tired. They managed to visit the small museum, before admitting defeat as Sasha and Bas tried to disguise their yawns.

The sun was setting as they drove home, the dusky countryside turning to molten gold and then finally to long evening shadows. Hayford Minster tower broke the skyline minutes before the sky began to sparkle with silver stars.

'Will you stay for supper?' Alissa asked as they drew up outside the house.

'I think not.' Max gestured to the back seat. The two children had fallen asleep, their heads drooped against the comfortable leather. 'But let me help you in with Sasha.'

They climbed out of the Discovery and Max opened the back door. He reached in for Sasha and drew her gently into his arms. In her half-sleep she nestled comfortably against his chest. Bas woke briefly, then snuggled down again, a small sigh escaping his lips.

Inside the house, the warmth of the day filled all the rooms. Silently, Alissa led the way upstairs and into Sasha's bedroom. Max lowered her to the bed and Alissa drew over the cover. For a moment they looked down at her, then Max walked softly to the door, turning briefly to glance and smile at Alissa as she followed him.

Back outside in the garden, mayflies were dancing on the chestnut leaves. The tops of the trees swayed above them, green and lush. The garden was peaceful and the brick of the house glowed in the last of the light.

'It's been a lovely day,' Alissa said as they stood at the gate.

'We never did have that talk.' His grey eyes looked down at her from under the dark pelt of hair, the warmth of his body reaching her, making her feel dizzy.

'Perhaps it was better that we didn't,' she responded quietly. 'After all, today was for the children's benefit.'

He nodded. 'I'd like to do this again some time. Would you?'

Alissa took a breath, unable to see the expression in his eyes. His voice was husky and soft. It had been a long time since she'd enjoyed herself so much. Although she could legitimately explain away their excursion as one made for Sasha's benefit, there was, she guessed, more to it than that. At the moment she didn't want to analyse her feelings. Neither did she welcome the responsibility of a commitment she might regret - just as she had done throughout the week.

'Think about it,' he said quietly, as though reading her mind. Then, without warning, he bent his head to brush his lips over hers. It was a swift gesture that caught her off guard. 'Goodnight,' he whispered as his warm breath flowed across her skin. 'Sleep well.'

She opened her mouth to reply but no words came. A few seconds later he turned on his heel and was striding away. Alone in the darkness and unable to move from the spot to which she seemed rooted, Alissa stood still, watching the taillights of the Discovery as they disappeared down the quiet road.

She watched until they were finally out of sight, her heart beating rapidly. At last she took a breath and turned back towards the house.

CHAPTER 5

❦

THE FOLLOWING MONDAY ALISSA wrote to Jamie and Betty Atkins. Before bringing up the subject of Emily with Max - or before Max approached her - she wanted to speak to Jamie. 'I would like Mr and Mrs Atkins to make an appointment with me,' she explained to Jane Barr, the practice secretary. 'I've drafted this.' She handed the letter to Jane. 'I've made it clear that I would like to see both of them together.'

Jane nodded. 'All right. I'll do it now and post it this evening. Would you like me to tell the reception girls that you're expecting the Atkinses to phone?'

'Yes, that might be an idea, Jane. Again, please, mention to them that I'd like to see Mrs *and* Mr Atkins.'

Jane laid the piece of paper in her tray, then frowned as she looked at the address. 'Are those the Atkinses of Poplar Farm?'

Alissa frowned. 'Yes. Do you know them?'

'I went to school with a girl called Di Slade and Betty Trowbridge, as she was then,' Jane said thoughtfully. 'How many children have the Atkinses got now?'

'Four,' said Alissa. 'And one on the way.'

Jane raised her eyebrows. 'So Betty got her football team in the end, did she?' Noticing Alissa's frown, she added, 'Children and marriage to Jamie was all she ever wanted. Betty had a crush on Jamie but he got engaged to Di. It was Betty really who broke them up. Betty got herself pregnant.'

'And Jamie was the father of the child?'

Jane nodded slowly. 'Di was broken-hearted and Jamie devastated. But Jamie did the honourable thing and married Betty. Di went off to be a stewardess and I also moved away. I've been back eighteen months now, but it's the first I've heard of Betty and Jamie, though I must say I'm not really surprised they are still at Poplar Farm. Betty always wanted to be a farmer's wife.'

Alissa was beginning to realise that there was a lot more to the Atkins story than she'd realised. Was Max aware of it? Jane hesitated and leaned her elbows on her desk, looking up at Alissa. 'The pity was, Jamie had decided to make a break from farming - he hated it really. His intention was to emigrate with Di to Australia. Then Betty announced her news.' Jane shrugged. 'Jamie's and Di's future changed overnight.'

Though she hated to admit it, Max had been right about the Atkins history being a complicated one. Alissa realised that Max's insistence that he talk to her regarding the Atkinses was probably justified and she regretted not having asked him more when she'd had the chance. As soon as an opportunity presented itself, she decided, she would bring up the matter again.

By Friday, the week had been so busy she had barely spoken to Max. Other than brief conversations shared in the company of others, they hadn't talked at any length. The new allergy clinic was in progress when Alissa's internal phone rang and roused her from her reflections.

'A Dr Hanson on the line for you, Alissa,' said Keeley Summers, one of the younger members of staff. 'Shall I put him through? He's ringing from Vancouver, Canada.'

'Yes,' said Alissa at once, 'and don't send anyone in for a minute or two, Keeley.'

Seconds later the deep voice of her brother-in-law reverberated over the line. 'Alissa—how are you?'

'Nick! I'm fine. This is a surprise.'

'Not a bad one, I hope?'

She laughed. 'No. It's always wonderful to hear from you.' Nick Hanson had been her late husband's half-brother and, despite sharing their mother's genes, they had been as different as chalk from cheese both in temperament and appearance. Alissa recalled with gratitude how Nick had flown from Canada to be by her side on the day of Mike's car crash. Without his support she doubted whether she would have coped through the nightmare.

'I'm due some leave very soon,' he told her uncertainly. 'I was thinking of flying over for a short break.'

Alissa knew him well enough to know that his voice revealed a thread of tension. Was his romance to beautiful television presenter Sherry Tate in trouble again? she wondered. 'That's wonderful news,' Alissa said with genuine enthusiasm. 'We've missed you, Nick.'

'How is Sash?' he asked, his tone once again cheerful. 'She'll be delighted to know her uncle Nick is flying over to see her,' Alissa assured him.

'I'm flying into Heathrow in early June. I'll fax you the dates later on. Then I'll book into a hotel'

'You certainly will not,' Alissa protested. 'Sasha and I will meet you at the airport - unless you have something in London you want to do?'

'Nothing special ... no.'

'Just let me know the details as soon as you can.' Alissa hesitated. 'Will Sherry be coming with you?'

'No, I'm afraid not. She's working away at the moment.'

Alissa sensed there was something wrong but their conversation was brought to an end by a knock on the door. As Keeley poked her head in, Alissa beckoned to her. 'I'm finished now,' she mouthed.

'Sorry to interrupt, Dr Leigh, but this young lady is in some distress.' A young teenager followed Keeley in.

Alissa nodded, made a signal with her hand and the girl sat down in the patient's chair. She said goodbye to Nick and glanced through the notes Keeley had left for her.

Clare Fardon, aged sixteen, was the first of a succession of patients that afternoon who were troubled by allergy problems and for whom Alissa prescribed antihistamine, recommending they attend the allergy clinic. The consultation took only a few moments and Clare left, clutching her prescription and blowing her nose. It was a sight that, Alissa reflected wryly, she would no doubt see many times over the next few months.

When the clinic was over, Alissa met Erin in the hallway. 'No problems?' Alissa asked, and Erin shook her head.

'The pollen count is high at the moment,' Erin commented, 'so it meant that almost everyone I saw had hay fever or a related allergy. The only one who didn't turn up was my young patient, Hannah Brent. She's eight and has a reaction to some foods. I suggested an elimination diet and was rather hoping to hear how she got on.' 'Perhaps Mo saw Hannah?' Alissa suggested.

Erin shook her head. 'No, I checked.'

'It might be a positive sign,' Alissa said optimistically, 'and Hannah's mother has worked out what the offending foods were.'

Erin didn't look convinced but all the same she nodded. 'Yes, perhaps.'

Walking into the office, Alissa saw Max, examining a large white card embossed with silver letters. He looked up and, smiling, handed the card to Alissa.

'I hope you can all come,' Erin said anxiously, looking from one to the other. 'Everyone at the practice is invited. That's why I asked Jane to leave the invitation in the office for the staff to see.'

Alissa read the details of Erin's wedding. Her eyes passed swiftly over the dainty silver lettering. 'The Minster?' she breathed. 'What a romantic place to have a wedding service.' She recalled how impersonal her own registry office wedding had seemed.

Erin blushed under her halo of thick chestnut hair. 'Simon's family wanted a service in London but luckily Simon understood how much it meant to me to be married in Hayford Minster.'

'Sensible chap,' said Max with a wry grin.

'We're having the reception at the Minster Court Hotel and there will be a disco in the evening, so I hope you'll all be able to stay for that, too.'

'Is the dress finished?' Alissa asked.

Erin nodded, it fits perfectly and the two bridesmaids - my sisters - are travelling over from Ireland for a fitting for theirs.' Erin took the card and placed it back on the desk. 'I'd better not start thinking too much about it - the prospect of all the family descending on my small flat is quite daunting.' She sighed. 'Well, I must leave for my calls. You're still in surgery, Alissa?'

Alissa nodded. 'I've a mum and toddlers clinic at four.' Erin grinned. 'All work and no play ...'

They laughed, but as Erin left Max turned to Alissa and crooked an eyebrow. 'Talking of play, I wondered if, for Sasha's birthday, you would consider a visit to the cinema? And before you answer, let me warn you that Bas and Sasha have concocted a scheme to persuade us. Only I thought it would be less painful for us if I discussed it with you first.' He laughed. 'Bas, I'm afraid, is hopeless at keeping secrets.'

Alissa frowned. 'Do you know what film it is?'

'A new Disney, I believe.' He gave her one of his crooked smiles. 'I just didn't want you to think I was the instigator of the idea - though, of course, I would be delighted if you could come.'

Alissa hesitated. Did she really want to make another date with Max, even though he was suggesting it was the children's idea? 'Well, I'll talk to Sasha this evening,' she said, and then thought of Nick. 'As it happens, I've some news of my own. Sasha's uncle is arriving from Canada to stay with us.'

'I see.' Max looked disappointed. 'Will that make any difference to your plans?'

'I'm not really sure at this point since I haven't the dates.' Alissa paused. She didn't want to get into an explanation about Nick, neither did she want to make any definite arrangements which might interfere with Nick's stay. 'I'll let you know a little closer to the time, if that's all right?'

'Perfectly.' His grey eyes wandered over her face as he added,

'Would you have a few minutes before your clinic to discuss Betty Atkins?'

Alissa nodded. 'Shall we try the staffroom?'

Max accompanied her there and they found it deserted. They made coffee and sat down, Max looking up thoughtfully as he twirled his spoon in the dark brown liquid. 'Have you seen either Betty or Jamie yet?' he asked her quietly.

'No, not yet, but I've written this morning to ask Betty and Jamie to come in together,' she told him as she sipped her drink. 'In fact, Betty may even turn up with the children this afternoon. I suggested she come to a clinic where the children could be occupied in the creche while we were talking.'

'Then it's important I tell you all I know,' Max said, laying his spoon in the saucer he was holding and looking up at her. 'I think it only fair that I put you in the picture about the Atkinses as Betty has singled you out for her attention. As I mentioned before, Jamie's opinion may differ from Betty's.'

'In what way?' Alissa asked. 'Has it something to do with the fact that Emily was once your patient?'

He nodded. 'Yes, for a while after Emily was diagnosed as autistic I treated her, but then Betty transferred to Erin. We had a minor difference of opinion - Betty said she would prefer to see a female doctor. She accused me of being prejudiced against her because I was male.'

Alissa sat forward. 'But that wasn't so, was it?'

'Of course not. But I had treated Jamie and knew his history. I was given to believe that Jamie was thrust into a situation with his marriage to Betty, but once they settled down I thought they had a fair chance of making a go of it. For some reason Betty got it into her mind that everyone was against her. I'd say it had become almost an obsession by the time Donna came along.'

'You believe she thought you were on Jamie's side and not hers?'

He nodded. 'Certainly Betty wasn't justified in her accusation of prejudice. I had hoped things might work out, but I can only conclude there's some deeper problem in their marriage. Hence my cause for concern regarding Emily. To my knowledge, Jamie is very close to the child. I think it important we tackle him, before making any major decisions.'

Alissa sat back and sighed, realising that indeed she had stumbled into a complex situation. Now that Max had explained it she could see that making a decision on Emily's future without Jamie's and Betty's mutual consent would be unwise to say the least.

'I wish I'd known all this before,' she said quietly. 'I wouldn't have let things run on so far.'

He nodded slowly. 'Until the practice meeting I'd no idea how deeply Betty had involved you. And then, when you said you hadn't seen Jamie, the warning bells sounded.'

His concerned stare made her cheeks burn. His voice was soft and apologetic, and as she looked at him he smiled, the same slow smile he had given her when he had bent his head to kiss her. She had tried to block that kiss from her mind but now, as she looked up at him, she saw the memory of it flare in his eyes.

Suddenly the phone rang and Max reached out to answer it. From the look on his face, Alissa knew instantly who it was. She met his eyes briefly, then the skin over his cheek-bones seemed to tighten and his broad shoulders stiffen. Priss couldn't have chosen a better moment, she thought with a pang of surprising - and uncharacteristic - irritation

CHAPTER 6

It was on a Monday at the very beginning of June that two very different young people walked into Alissa's consulting room. The girl, who was eighteen according to her temporary records, wore a rather grubby long skirt and had dark, braided hair. Accompanying her was a young man who looked very thin and had a sallow, slightly yellow complexion. Their fifteen-month-old baby, carried by the girl, clung to her neck and grizzled softly.

'We're travellers,' announced the young woman, who called herself India, 'and we don't usually need doctors. But something's wrong with Orion - '

'We use our own medicines and herbs,' interrupted the young man, who gave his name as Sky. 'They told us we had to get Orion vaccinated for measles and we don't believe in it. Some friends of ours had their baby done and he started to have fits. We don't want that happening to Orion.'

Alissa glanced at the few details she had of Orion's medical history. 'But you have had the DTP and polio immunisations?'

'We didn't have a choice,' replied India. 'We were living with my mother when Orion was young. She said all babies had to be immunised, but we've been travelling for three months now and when Orion has been sick we've cured him ourselves.'

'Except for the problem down here,' added Sky. He removed his son's nappy and Alissa saw that one of the tiny testes was swollen.

'How long has Orion had this problem?' she asked as she examined the child.

'About a week,' said his mother. 'And it's painful sometimes. But he's had his herbs this morning and he seems a bit better.'

Alissa saw at once that Orion's testis had not properly descended into the scrotum and that no amount of herbs would help the little boy's condition. She was also concerned at the attitude of the two young people regarding the measles immunisation. Aware that she must attend to the most serious matter first, she began to write out a hospital form.

'Orion will need to be seen by a specialist,' she explained carefully. 'I'll make an appointment for you straight away - '

'We aren't going to any hospitals,' objected the young man at once. 'They only make things worse.'

'Orion's testis should have descended during his first year of life,' Alissa pointed out, 'and it must be surgically untwisted to restore the blood flow.'

'Won't it untwist on its own?' India asked.

'Not now.' Alissa looked at them both. 'It could have done earlier in his life, but if the problem isn't rectified now, apart from considerable pain for Orion, there will be many more related problems.'

'We've cured his sickness before,' the young man interrupted at once, 'with our own medicine. We could do it again.'

'I doubt that very much.' Alissa was firm now. 'Fortunately Orion doesn't seem to be in any discomfort at the moment, but left untreated he may have severe pain.' Alissa finally convinced the young woman, if not her partner, that they must take Orion for specialist treatment. Phoning the hospital there and then, she arranged for the family to be seen swiftly. When they had gone, she sat for a moment, frowning at the information she had managed to extricate and write on the temporary records in front of her.

What was worrying was that the family would move on again. Their caravan, among a number of others, was parked illegally in a field on the outskirts of Hayford Minster. It was only a matter of time before the authorities forced them to leave. It was a problem she was still mulling over when Jane knocked on her door and walked in. 'This fax came for you,' she told Alissa.

Alissa glanced at it. 'Thanks, Jane. It's from my brother-in-law, Nick Hanson. He's coming to stay for a while and these look like his arrival dates.'

'I couldn't help noticing he's a doctor,' Jane said hesitantly. 'Is he coming to work in the UK?'

'Oh, no. This break is just a holiday.'

'A pity,' sighed Jane, raising her eyebrows. 'Alec is desperate to get away for a week at about that time to a medical convention, but with things as they are - with Erin having her two weeks off right in the middle of summer for her wedding - it doesn't look like he'll make it.'

'And you were thinking that Nick might locum for us?'

Jane smiled ruefully. 'The thought had crossed my mind.'

Alissa wondered if Nick would be interested. 'I'll email him rather than phone this evening, Jane,' Alissa decided. 'Then he can give it some thought.'

'Thanks, that would be a real help,' Jane said with a grin. 'I know Kirstie would be delighted. It will be one headache less for her this morning.' Kirstie James was the practice manager and she had just returned from holiday to be met with a backlog of work.

Alissa nodded. 'But don't mention it yet. Let me contact Nick first.'

Jane agreed and once on her own again Alissa turned her attention back to her list. She glanced at the records of baby Orion and put them to one side. On her way home this evening, she would pass the travellers' camp. Not that she could do very much, but she would satisfy herself that they hadn't already flown the nest.

Over the next few days, Alissa's fears were allayed. The travellers hadn't moved on and she had seen the dark head of Sky emerging from one of the caravans. Her other concern, Nick's response to her email, was also dealt with as Nick replied immediately that he would be delighted to locum for Alec.

Max proved to be the only stumbling block of the week when on Friday night, before leaving surgery, he stopped to talk to her in the car park.

'Have you heard anything from the Atkinses yet?' he asked, leaning against her white Ford.

'No, I'm afraid not.' Alissa sighed. 'I don't quite see what else I can do.'

'We could call at the farm together,' he suggested.

She hesitated. 'Wouldn't that seem rather like joining forces?'

He shrugged. 'Yes, but then we might get a response.'

'What about your past upset with Betty?'

'I'm still Jamie's doctor - officially,' he said, lifting his dark eyebrows. 'There's no reason why I shouldn't approach him.'

Alissa thought about it and said, 'Let's give it one more week. If we haven't heard from them by then, we'll do as you suggest.'

The June evening was beautiful, everything still bathed in sunshine, and as he leaned back against the car, his grey eyes seemed to hold her in their thrall. It was a perfect evening and she wished for a moment that she wasn't going home. It was a ridiculous thought because she was tired. It was the end of the week and she had been on call for several nights.

Astrid was flying to Sweden for three days which meant that the next few hours would be hectic, driving Astrid to the coach station and returning to make a meal. Sasha was bringing home a friend to stay on Saturday night as a birthday treat. On Sunday they were driving to Heathrow to collect Nick from the airport.

But standing here in the calm, warm air, talking to Max, she felt reluctant to depart. He, too, seemed unwilling to leave as, looking down at the tips of his shoes over his folded arms, he began to speak.

'I wonder if you had any thoughts on that film we discussed? Or rather that Bas and Sasha seemed keen to see. It's Sasha's birthday on Monday, isn't it?'

Sasha had mentioned it several times now and Alissa nodded. 'Do you still want to go?'

He grinned. 'Wild horses wouldn't stop me. I've almost forgotten what popcorn tastes like.' They laughed and he added quietly, 'There's an evening performance from six to eight.'

Alissa smiled wryly. 'You're very well informed.'

His grey eyes twinkled. 'And I thought, as I'm off duty earlier than you, I could collect the two of them from school, take them home and feed them - courtesy of Mrs Dunphy. We could then call for you here at a quarter to six.'

The suggestion certainly had its appeal, Alissa reflected, as Astrid would be away until Monday evening. To have Sasha collected and fed would help with her schedule. She was tempted to agree when she suddenly remembered Nick.

'I'm driving to Heathrow to collect my brother-in-law on Sunday,' she explained hesitantly. 'I've left Monday evening free ...'

Max nodded. 'Alec told me he's acting as locum for the week Alec's away. I'm looking forward to meeting him. Why not ask him to join us?'

'Well, yes, I suppose I could, though I'm not sure if he's a Disney fan. You see, Nick is unmarried - he has no children, but he's a wonderful uncle to Sasha and ...' She paused. 'Nick was a great support to us when my husband died.'

There was a brief silence as Max gazed at her, his eyes intent on her face. 'I'm sorry,' he apologised. 'You must have a lot to discuss. Perhaps it would be as well to leave the movies until another time.' He levered himself away from the car and, lifting his case, he slid his hand in his trouser pocket to find his keys. 'Have a good trip on Sunday,' he said quietly, and climbed into the Discovery.

By the time Alissa had time to think what had happened, she was watching the vehicle move past her, the crunch of gravel and the diesel throb of the engine fading into the distance.

She opened her car door and sank into the front seat, leaving the window open to allow in the cool evening air. Why had she refused Max's suggestion? No doubt Nick would enjoy a movie and, had she thought, she could have prepared a small supper afterwards, thus making Sasha's birthday a special one.

Now she would have to abandon all idea of the movie for obviously they couldn't go if Max still intended to take Bas. She would not only disappoint Sasha but have made a simple arrangement into a complicated one.

Somewhere in the fields beyond, a thrush warbled its beautiful summer song. The air was soft and sweet, refreshing to inhale. There were no more patients to see - she wasn't on duty over the weekend. Nick was arriving on Sunday, the only remaining relative either she or Sasha had. She should be feeling happy and full of anticipation, but her conversation with Max had cast a cloud over all that.

As she drove home she realised why. It was because she was attracted to Max and because she wanted - more than anything now that she had avoided it - to spend time with him. When he had kissed her he had woken something inside her. Despite all logic and common sense, and knowing that he was still involved with Priss, how could she be contemplating a relationship with him?

She had experienced a shared love with Mike. It had been almost worse than no love at all. But what if Max wasn't still involved with Priss? an uncertain voice inside asked her. Could she be certain that Priss was still part of his life - his future?

'You idiot, Alissa Leigh,' she murmured to herself as she glanced at her pleated brow in the driving mirror. 'What are you thinking of?'

Max probably had no more intention of embarking on a relationship with her than of flying to Mars. He was merely asking her and Sasha, very politely, if they would like to see a movie. A Disney film. What possible harm could there be in that? He had even suggested that Nick should join them. At the Minster, Alissa glanced swiftly to her right and left, turned into the narrow lane that offered a short cut home and wondered if she had the courage to phone Max when she arrived there.

CHAPTER 7

A RED MERCEDES was parked in front of the house as Alissa turned into her drive. Astrid and Sasha were standing on the lawn in conversation with a tall, dark-haired man wearing shorts, a sweater slung casually over his shoulder.

As she climbed out of her car Sasha ran towards her. 'Mummy, Uncle Nick's here. Look what he's brought for me from Canada!' Breathlessly Sasha stopped to pull out the hem of her new sweatshirt. 'Bears live in this forest,' gurgled Sasha excitedly, pointing to the illustration of high mountains and a lake, 'and there are whales and seals and - '

'Slow down, sweetheart.' Alissa laughed softly. 'Let me say hello to Uncle Nick first.'

Alissa looked up to see her brother-in-law striding towards her. In seconds she found herself in a warm embrace. 'Nick!' She hugged his tall, muscular frame. 'But you're not supposed to be here until Sunday!'

He laughed as he released her. 'I got away from work earlier than I thought so I jumped an earlier flight and hired a car at Heathrow. Thought I'd save you the long haul up to London. I hope this is convenient?'

'Of course it is. It's wonderful to see you. How long have you been here?'

'A couple of hours. Astrid fed and watered me and Sasha has shown me around. You really have a great house here.'

Alissa recalled the last time Nick had been in England. They'd been living in the old house which had incorporated the practice she'd shared with Mike and Alec Rogers on the outskirts of the town. After Mike's funeral she had told Nick in her letters about her intended move, but they hadn't moved into Green Gables until after his last visit to England. As they walked back towards Astrid, with Sasha's hand tucked firmly into her uncle's, Alissa felt a warm glow of pride. Green Gables was a lovely house and her choice. She hoped Nick would approve and that his stay in England would be happy - despite Sherry's absence.

CHAPTER 8

'A LOT HAS HAPPENED in the past year. I don't know quite where to begin,' Alissa found herself explaining later that evening as they sat quietly in the garden, talking. Nick had driven Astrid to the bus station, Sasha was fast asleep in bed and the house was quiet. They had finished supper and had adjourned to the swing seat, indulging in a mellow wine Nick had brought with him.

'Tell me about the new practice,' Nick murmured, a smile tugging at the corners of his mouth. 'Then I'll tell you my news.'

Alissa nodded as she leaned her head back on the seat. It felt good to talk to Nick again. He was part of her past and she could talk freely to him as she always had throughout their long friendship.

By the time they went back indoors they had covered most topics, though one was touched on only briefly - that of Sherry, his fiancee. Alissa sensed that he was reticent on the subject, preferring to tell her about his own work in general practice in Vancouver.

It was only when the evening was over and it was time for bed that Alissa remembered that she'd intended to telephone Max, explaining she'd changed her mind about the movie. As she slid down between the cool cotton sheets and lay there, thinking about the day, she wondered if she should simply let the matter drop.

Surprised at her own feeling of disappointment at this thought, she closed her eyes and decided to leave all decisions until the morning. It wasn't easy, she discovered as Max's dark features and grey eyes seemed to appear in her mind even on the borders of sleep.

Summoning up her courage on Monday morning, Alissa knocked on Max's door before surgery began.

'Max, have you a few minutes free?' she asked as she opened the door to his call, his deep voice echoing across the room.

He stood up and, smiling, gestured to the chair beside his desk. 'Of course. Come in.'

She took the seat and, aware of his curious gaze on her face, lifted her eyes to his. 'This may sound silly,' she faltered, 'but I wonder if I could change my mind about this evening?'

'You mean the movie?' he asked in surprise.

She nodded. 'You are still going to see it?'

'Oh, yes,' he said quietly, resting back in his chair, a thoughtful expression on his face. 'Do you mind if I ask what brought about the change of mind?'

'Nick arrived unexpectedly on Friday,' she began to explain, 'and we've had plenty of time to catch up on news. In fact, he's off to see some friends for the day ... and so ... ' Max was silent then leaned forward and, studying her face. 'And so that leaves you free?'

'Well, yes...it does.'

'All the same, I had the impression on Friday you weren't keen to go,' he said, arching a quizzical eyebrow. 'At least not with Bas and me.'

His directness caught her by surprise. 'I'm sorry if I gave you that idea. I simply didn't want to make an arrangement with you and then have to break it.'

'You needn't have worried.' He shrugged, his eyes not leaving her face.

A shiver of awareness ran down her spine as he seemed to be reading her mind - and, possibly, the truth. 'As I said, I didn't want to encroach.' Alissa met his gaze. 'I merely thought we could enjoy another outing as before - with no strings attached, as it were. Like you, the events of the past have discouraged me from expecting a perfect world. If you'd cancelled at the last minute it wouldn't have been a disaster.'

Feeling as though she were back at school and being duly admonished for bad homework, Alissa swallowed. Whatever thoughts she'd had after that kiss, Max had dispelled them by that last levelling statement.

'Is that a yes?' she asked uncertainly.

'Why not?' He gave her a small smile and rose to his feet. 'Have you made any arrangements for collecting Sasha from school?'

'No, not yet. Astrid is away until this evening and Nick is in London. I was about to telephone a friend whose daughter is in the same class as Sasha. Occasionally we call on one another for lifts.'

'Would it be any help if we reverted to my original suggestion?' he said easily. 'Mrs Dunphy would be delighted to do the honours for tea. Then you can come straight to my house from the surgery. All you need do is phone the school and let them know I shall be collecting Sasha.'

'Are you sure?' she asked uncertainly.

He gave her an amused smile. 'Oh, I think I'll be able to manage that.'

Back in her room she sat down at her desk and expelled a long breath. She placed her palms on her hot cheeks and for a moment closed her eyes, letting the silence of the room wash over her. However had she managed to make things so complicated for herself? Had Max suspected her true reason for not accepting his offer in the first place? Or was his indifferent manner a natural reaction to her indecisiveness?

If the latter was the case, Alissa reflected as she picked up the phone to ring Sasha's school, then she may have lost a little pride but he hadn't guessed at the truth. And the truth was hard, even for her, to accept. She *wanted* to be in his company; she had felt a sharp stab of disappointment at the prospect of not being with him. And despite all she knew of his relationship with his ex-wife, she was allowing herself to give in to the attraction she felt for him.

The headmistress's voice came over the line and, clearing her throat, Alissa explained that Max would be collecting Sasha from school.

That afternoon, Alissa saw Max's Discovery move slowly out of the car park. It was just after three and from where she stood in the office, gazing out of the window, she was able to watch the vehicle as it disappeared into the narrow road leading to Minster Square.

To all intents and purposes, she should be relieved at Max's earlier comments. After all, that was what she had wanted at first, wasn't it? No commitment on a personal level, but a good working partnership and a few shared outings. Now, however, that in some way had changed. What was Max's relationship with his ex-wife? Given that Priss seemed to be still part of his life, surely she had to assume that they could still be together?

'Alissa?' Lyn Hall's voice broke into her thoughts and she turned from the window.

'Yes ... what is it, Lyn?'

'I'm not sure, exactly,' said the receptionist, glancing cautiously over her shoulder. 'Trouble, I think.'

'With whom?'

'Well, it's Aaron Darvill.'

'Max's son?'

Lyn nodded. 'He came to see his father but Dr Darvill has just left. Do you know if Dr Darvill's going straight home?'

'As a matter of fact, he isn't,' Alissa replied. Walking towards Lyn, she glanced into the corridor. 'Max is going to Bas's school. Do you know what the problem is?'

'I would guess he's had a quarrel with his mother from the little he's said,' Lyn said in a low tone. 'It looks to me as if he's been crying. He managed to cover it up well enough, but I've got two teenagers of my own and I know all the signs. I don't really feel happy about letting him go off in that state.'

Alissa lifted her eyebrows. 'I see.' Almost as though to echo her earlier thoughts, it seemed that Priss was never very far away. She looked at Lyn. 'I'll speak to him if you like.'

'Oh, thanks, Dr Leigh.' Lyn looked relieved and accompanied her to the waiting room where Aaron Darvill was sitting on a chair, his blond hair falling over his face, his backpack wedged between his booted feet.

He looked up, his blue eyes red-rimmed, though he made an effort to smile. 'Hello, Dr Leigh. I was looking for Dad.'

Alissa had met Max's elder son several times over the past six months. He was a typical modern teenager and, unlike shy Bas, healthily outgoing. But today he looked far from happy, his manner withdrawn, and Lyn's observation had been astute, Alissa thought. The boy had been weeping.

Lyn went back to the desk and Alissa explained that Max was collecting the children from school.

'Oh, well, I suppose it'll have to wait,' Aaron muttered, obviously disappointed.

'Is there anything I can do to help?' Alissa asked.

He stood up and, dragging his bag over his shoulder, shrugged. 'No, not really. I just had to tell Dad something. It doesn't matter.'

'You've only just missed him. He's gone to school to collect Bas and Sasha.' Alissa watched him hesitate then was surprised when he looked up at her and said, 'It's just that Mum's at home. I finished school early and she was there when I got in. I thought ... well, I thought I'd better let Dad know.'

'Are you going home now?' Alissa asked, wondering what she should do.

He shook his blond head. 'Not yet, I don't s'pose. I'll walk around for a bit.' Avoiding eye contact with Alissa, he turned away.

'Aaron, wait a moment.' She paused, wondering if she was doing the right thing, then decided that no harm could come of what she was about to suggest and it would certainly be better than allowing him to go off with nowhere to go. 'I've an idea,' she said, signalling him to follow her. 'Just come into my room for a minute, will you?' Reluctantly he followed her and, once in her room, Alissa took her bag and brought out her purse. She slipped her front-door key from the brass ring on which she kept her car keys and handed it to him.

'You know where I live,' she told him. 'Go in and make yourself at home. Your father and I are taking Bas and Sasha to the movies, so you'll have the house to yourself. Make a coffee and a sandwich if you're hungry. Have you any project work from school?'

He nodded. 'Yeah ... quite a bit.'

'There's a laptop in my study. Go ahead and use it. There's no password so you can log straight in.'

She saw a look of relief creep over his face. 'That's cool. Dr Leigh. But what about Dad?'

'I'll ring him if you like and let him know where you are.'

Aaron nodded and took the key, looking a good deal happier than a few minutes previously.

Lynn sent in her first patient, and it wasn't until after she'd seen the woman - a brief consultation for a BP check, that she telephoned Max.

To her relief, she heard Max's voice come over the line. She guessed, from the tension in it, that Priss was there. 'I thought it best to let you know Aaron was at the surgery a short while ago,' she said, going on to explain what had happened.

He was clearly relieved that Aaron was accounted for. 'Thank you,' he said quietly. 'I was worried about him.'

'Can you cope with the children or would you like me to come and collect Sasha?' she asked before she rang off.

'No,' he told her firmly. 'The children are fine. They are with Mrs Dunphy in the garden, having a picnic tea.' 'And our arrangement still stands?' she asked. 'Or would you prefer to collect Aaron?'

'Not at all,' he replied without hesitation. 'I'll see you, as arranged, when you leave work. And, Alissa ...?'

'Yes?'

'I'm in your debt once again.'

Alissa replaced the phone with a sigh, reflecting that however hard she tried to avoid becoming involved in Max's life she hadn't succeeded.

Despite finishing her surgery on time, and eager to leave, Lyn asked her if she would be prepared to see a late arrival. 'The girl's come from school,' Lyn told her. 'Said it was her only chance to get here.'

Alissa sat down at her desk again and a few seconds later Lyn opened her door and ushered in Clare Fardon.

'Hello, Clare.' Alissa gestured to the chair. 'How are the hay-fever problems?'

The girl sat, but her face was white and she looked distinctly uncomfortable. 'It's not the hay fever I've come about,' she told Alissa hesitantly. 'It's something else.' Alissa waited, but her patient merely bit on her lip and looked down into her lap, apparently reluctant to explain her visit. Alissa studied the clear blue eyes and long fair hair drawn back into a band, noting the way Clare twisted her fingers nervously in her lap.

'I want to go on the Pill,' she said eventually, meeting Alissa's gaze.

Alissa glanced at the notes on her desk. 'You're just sixteen, Clare?'

Clare nodded, frowning at Alissa. 'All my friends are on it already. Some of them aren't even sixteen yet.'

'Is that why you want to use a contraceptive Pill - because of its popularity?'

Clare hesitated. 'I've got a boyfriend. He - we - well, both of us don't want to risk anything if we ... you know. And I s'pose it's the only alternative.' Her voice tailed off and she dropped her head again.

Alissa wasn't altogether convinced that her young patient was enthusiastic about her request for the Pill. 'Clare, taking the Pill at your age carries a lot of responsibility,' Alissa said gently. 'Although I know you are trying to be sensible, the first step is to make sure that you and your boyfriend really do want to commit to a relationship.'

'It's not like that,' Clare retorted sharply. 'It's ... not like a heavy relationship.' She saw Alissa's frown of concern. 'You don't understand, no one does. Boys don't go in for that sort of thing any more. They won't go out with you if you don't, well, if you don't want sex.'

'But what about you, Clare? You have your own opinion on the subject. I'm sure.'

The girl's eyes filled with tears. 'But there's no other choice, is there? What if something happened? My parents would kill me. And my boyfriend's dad would ...' She stopped, shaking her head as the tears threatened to flow.

'All parents are worried for their children.' Alissa tried to reason with the girl. 'It's only natural, Clare. They love you and want the best for you.'

'My dad is a policeman,' Clare said thickly, 'so it's even worse for me than other girls. And my boyfriend's father is ...' She brought her eyes up to meet Alissa's stare.

'Is what, Clare?' Alissa prompted.

'I can't say.' Clare looked down and twisted her fingers anxiously in her lap again.

'Clare, may I make a suggestion? Bring your boyfriend to see me and then we can discuss this together.'

'No! He can't - we can't! Don't you see?' Clare stood up and, grabbing hold of her schoolbag, shook her head fiercely. 'If he did that, he'd -' The girl bit her lip, as though preventing herself from confessing to something she would later regret. Then, with a sob, she rushed to the door and fled from the room.

Startled, Alissa hurried after her, but by the time she arrived in Reception there was no sign of her young patient. Dismayed that she had failed to help, Alissa returned to her room. There was little more she could do, she decided reluctantly, until Clare contacted her again - if she contacted her again.

As she gathered her things and walked to Reception the thought crossed her mind that she might try to reach Clare at her home. There was a telephone number on her records, but if one of her parents answered it would be impossible to explain the reason for Clare's visit. As Clare had probably not told her parents she was coming here today, the call could only do more harm than good.

Alissa decided she would have to wait, hoping that Clare would reflect on what had been said and make a further appointment to see her.

Saying goodnight to Ruth and Lyn, Alissa hurried out to her car. By the time she arrived at Max's house it was almost six.

'You're late, Mummy,' Sasha complained as she opened the door to her mother's knock. Alissa had visited Max's house once before at the beginning of the year. Then it had been to attend an informal meeting of the partners as the practice had made its debut in Hayford Minster.

Now, the rambling old house, in daylight, looked less austere, with two boys' bikes propped in the hall amidst a pile of football boots and rucksacks.

'Sorry, darling,' Alissa apologised, bending down to kiss her daughter, 'but better late than never.'

'Dr Darvill collected me and Bas from school today,' Sasha said shyly. 'Because it was my birthday. And Mrs Dunphy made us tea and helped me change into my clean things and -'

'Hello, Dr Leigh,' called Bas as he hurtled down the stairs after Sasha. He was trying to pull on a sweater, his newly washed face flushed with excitement. 'Dad says he's almost ready and to ask if you want a cup of tea.'

Alissa smiled gratefully. 'No, thanks, Bas. Perhaps we'll have a drink at the cinema.'

A moment or two later Max hurried down the stairs. He was dressed in jeans and a fawn collarless shirt which accentuated his deep tan. His hair was smoothed back and looked thick and glossy against the chiselled features of his handsome face. He gave Alissa a welcoming smile. 'All set?'

She nodded, momentarily wishing she, too, could have changed her clothes, but fortunately the slim-fitting pale green dress she had put on this morning wasn't creased despite the day's activity. Had Clare Fardon not arrived at the last moment she might have had the opportunity to change at work. She always kept a spare set of clothing for emergencies, but Alissa supposed it didn't really matter. Everyone seemed too excited to notice her appearance.

The Disney film was all it had been reported to be. The sound effects and animation held everyone spellbound. Because they had indulged in only one tub of popcorn Max took them out to supper at a restaurant afterwards. The evening was full of fun and laughter and, having ravenously devoured four pizza specials, they left the restaurant for home.

By the time they arrived back at Max's house it was dusk and the children stifled their yawns as they sat together on the rear seat. 'Can we all go to the cinema again?' Bas asked in a sleepy voice as his father turned the Discovery into the drive.

'We'll see,' Max answered vaguely, about to open his door.

'It's much more fun with Bas, Mummy,' said Sasha on a yawn. 'It's like having a brother.'

An awkward silence descended as Max hesitated. Pushing open his door, he glanced briefly at Alissa. When Bas had been safely escorted indoors Sasha was ferried to the back seat of Alissa's Ford, where she soon fell asleep.

Max leaned against the car and grinned.

'We do seem to have enjoyed ourselves,' he murmured. 'At least I know I did.'

'Yes, me, too.' She glanced at her watch. 'I'll drive Aaron home this evening. Astrid will be back by then and will wait with Sasha until I get back.'

He frowned. 'I'm afraid I haven't had a chance to explain about Aaron. Did he tell you he had a quarrel with his mother today?'

Alissa nodded. 'I guessed something like that must have happened.'

'It seems to happen more frequently these days,' Max sighed, his grey eyes narrowed as he looked down at the ground.

'Perhaps because he's growing up quickly,' Alissa said. 'The teenage years aren't easy.'

Max looked up and she saw his eyes were tired now, the excitement of the evening passing and leaving him distracted once more. 'Naturally, I feel responsible,' he said quietly. 'I had hoped that the boys would adjust to the divorce, but even though it's been six years now there are still problems. I go along with much of what Priss wants just to keep the peace. Given the choice, things would be very different.'

It was the first time he had spoken so intimately of his relationship with Priss. Was it the truth? she wondered.

'I wish it could be different,' he added regretfully, 'but Bas is very young. I want his life to be as normal as possible, not easy when his mother appears without warning. I'm afraid I've just had to accept that over the years, for the boys' sake.'

Alissa looked at him and wondered if he was really being honest with himself. She wanted to believe that what he had told her was true and that he wasn't still using the boys as an excuse to maintain links with Priss. But she had trusted before, had believed that her husband had finally finished with the woman with whom he had had an affair, only to learn that he was still seeing her. And she recalled how painful that had been, how the memory of it still had the power to hurt her. Was Max like Mike? Was he unable to turn away from the woman he loved?

Alissa suddenly felt cold and she shivered. Max eased himself away from the car and looked down at her. 'You're cold - and it's late.'

'It's been a lovely evening, Max.'

'Goodnight,' he said softly. Reaching out to place his hands on her shoulders, he bent his head, his mouth coming down to close over hers. She responded to his kiss, her heart beating fast as she opened her lips to his soft enquiry. His kiss was sweet and brought back the memory of the first time, though now there was something added, an intimacy which left her wanting more.

Then, being aware of the children, he drew away, his hands sliding down her arms to her wrists to which he applied soft pressure as his grey eyes flared slightly before releasing her.

They were silent, standing in the dusk, and Alissa realised that neither of them wanted the evening to end.

'Goodnight,' he whispered.

She smiled softly and he opened the car door for her. She climbed in and started the engine, looking up at him briefly before pulling out of the drive.

On their way home, Sasha woke and sat up, yawning. 'Dr Darvill's really nice,' she said sleepily.

Alissa smiled in the mirror. 'Yes, I suppose he is.'

'Is he your boyfriend, Mummy?'

Alissa looked in the mirror again. 'Whatever made you say that?'

'Aaron's mummy wanted to take Aaron and Bas to meet her new

boyfriend. But Aaron doesn't want to meet Claude, nor does Bas - and, anyway, Dr Darvill told her that we were all going out to the cinema and it wasn't con - cov - '

'Convenient,' said Alissa, surprised at what her daughter was telling her.

'Mrs Dunphy made us some pancakes and we took them out to the treehouse. It was brilliant. Mum, can I have a treehouse, too?'

'We'll see,' said Alissa distractedly.

'That's what all grown-ups say,' said Sasha, yawning. 'It really means no.'

The house lights were on when they arrived and Aaron appeared at the front door, his rucksack on his back. 'I saw your headlights from the living room,' he explained as they climbed out of the car. 'Happy birthday, Sasha. Did you like the movie?'

'It was brilliant,' began Sasha, intent on describing the film from beginning to end. Fortunately she was stopped by the appearance of Astrid who held out her hand and called her.

'Bye, Aaron!' Sasha skipped past him shyly.

'Thanks a lot for tonight, Dr Leigh,' Aaron said as Alissa drove him home despite protests that he wanted to walk.

'You're welcome, Aaron.'

'Is Dad cool about today?' he asked after a while.

Alissa nodded and turned briefly to smile at him. 'He'll be pleased to see you.' She waved to him as he slammed the door and jogged up the drive. Max's house, like hers, looked cosy and inviting, the downstairs windows brightly lit and radiating light into the darkness.

That night, before she climbed into bed, she sat quietly, thinking about the events of the day. Max, it appeared, had not been deterred from his plans by Priss, added to which he had shed some light on what had puzzled her before the fact that he went along with his ex-wife for the sake of the children and no other reason.

As she laid her head on the pillow, she allowed herself to recall the expression in his eyes as he'd kissed her, dark and intense. Her body had shivered at his touch. There had been other times, too, which she recalled - once in the cinema, above the children's heads, his face turned towards her, his smile slow and intimate. Another, when his laughter had echoed across and caught at something in her heart. In the restaurant, as the children had amused them with their remarks about the film, they had exchanged a fleeting glance as they'd both looked up at each other and known what the other was thinking.

She found herself trying hard to recall any such moments in her marriage as she drifted on the borderland of |sleep. But she could remember very few family outings. Mike had always promised that one day it would be different - they would spend time together, indulge in the, family lifestyle she had always dreamed of. He had offered her so much when she'd met him and yet there had been so little family life to remember him by. A fierce dart of anger woke her briefly from sleep. He had found time for his mistress and not for her or Sasha. She felt the hot tears well behind her eyes. After all these years she could still be hurt by a memory! Then, as though her body's internal defence mechanism took over, the pain ceased. She closed her eyes and, remembering another man's face and the silvery, shimmering image of his gaze as he'd kissed her, she drifted into sleep.

CHAPTER 9

It was a week later when Nick began to help at the surgery. That same Monday morning, Annie Partridge walked into Alissa's room. Alissa had just completed her surgery and, gulping a cup of coffee, was about to sign the last prescription.

'I thought this might help Betty.' Annie handed the slim paper folder to Alissa. 'It's the report I promised.'

Alissa smiled. 'Thanks, Annie, but at the moment I'm no closer to sorting out an answer for Emily.'

'She's a dear little girl.' Annie remarked thoughtfully. 'Just needs that extra bit of attention.'

'Yes.' agreed Alissa on a sigh. 'We'll see what we can do.'

'Let me know if I can help,' Annie said as she left.

Almost immediately Keeley Summers came in. 'Dr Leigh. I know you've finished but there's a person just arrived calling herself India. She says it's urgent that she talks to you. Will you see her?'

'India?' Alissa nodded. 'We should have some temporary records for this young woman - see what you can find for me, Keeley, will you?'

'Under that name?'

Alissa smiled wryly. 'Yes, it's all we've got at the moment.'

After a while the young girl with dreadlocks came into the room and Alissa gestured towards the chair. 'How's Orion?' she asked as her patient sat down.

'He's in hospital,' India said quietly. Alissa could see mauve patches beneath her eyes, masked by her long fringe. 'They're operating on him this morning.'

Alissa consulted the file on her computer that Keeley sent through.

'I wanted to attend that first appointment, I really did,' India continued. 'But Sky said the hospital would just fill him up with drugs and he would get an infection like our friend's baby did. He said it was best for us to take him home and give him some more herbs.'

'But herbs wouldn't have helped,' Alissa emphasised. Sighing, she shook her head as she sank back in her chair. 'You'd better tell me what happened.'

India pushed her hand across her eyes. 'Orion started screaming in the middle of the night. I thought it might be something to do with his problem, but Sky disagreed. He kept trying to give him something he'd made up from herbs.' She blinked tearfully as she looked up, running her fingers across her wet lashes. 'I didn't know what to do. In the end I took him myself in the morning and gave consent for Orion to have the operation. We had an awful argument and Sky left. I ran after him and he hasn't shown up at the caravan since.'

'You do know that without an operation the implications for Orion would have been very serious?' Alissa looked at her steadily.

India nodded. 'But what am I going to do without Sky?'

'He'll come home,' Alissa said quietly. 'He's probably just letting off steam.'

'But he was so mad at me for signing that form.'

'You did the right thing,' Alissa assured her. 'Don't worry about him. He'll come home when he realises his mistake.'

India shook her head miserably, then rose to her feet. 'I'd better get back to the hospital.'

Alissa saw how weary she was and picked up her case. 'Come on, it's my lunch-hour. I'll drive you back to the caravan and we'll see if he's there. Then I'll take you back to the hospital.'

But Sky wasn't at the travellers' camp. They checked the caravan and India's neighbours but no one had seen Sky. Eventually Alissa drove her back to the hospital and, having attempted to reassure her, watched the thin, lonely figure walk dejectedly into the building.

When Alissa returned to the surgery she met Nick in the car park. Still preoccupied by thoughts of India and her troubles, Alissa gave him a cheerful smile. 'How did your first morning go?' she asked.

'Oh, I think I came through unscathed.' Nick propped an elbow on the roof of the Mercedes and, pushing his dark hair back over his head with his palm, he grinned. 'But it was only thanks to Erin or I might never have seen the light of day again. You'll probably understand when I say I had a visit from a certain Mr Freshwater.'

Alissa raised her eyebrows. 'Oh, dear, what was it this time?'

'Fracture of the femur.' Nick tried hard to keep a straight face. 'Or, failing that, avascular necrosis.'

Alissa smiled ruefully. 'I saw Mr Freshwater on Saturday, running rings around the staff in Sainsbury's. He didn't appear to have a broken hip then.'

'A point which Erin tactfully made when she interrupted our extended consultation.'

Nick began to chuckle. 'One of the reception staff told her I might need some help. Does he really plough alphabetically through the medical dictionary?'

Alissa joined in with his amusement. 'I'm afraid he came with us as part of the furniture from the old surgery. Luckily, he's quite happy once you've talked him out of the illness. It's rather time-consuming, I'm afraid.'

'You can say that again! He certainly reads up on his medicine. It was a relief to see Erin's friendly face.' Alissa smiled, noting her brother-in-law's expression as he talked of Erin.

'I understand,' murmured Nick, raising an eyebrow, 'that Erin is about to be wed to someone called Simon Forester, a high flyer, by the sound of it, in the City.'

'You're very well informed,' Alissa teased.

He grinned. 'I managed to persuade her into a pub lunch after my debacle with Mr Freshwater. I played for sympathy and, luckily, got it.' He added after a pause, 'And then I found myself telling her all about Sherry.'

Alissa looked up in surprise. Over the past few days Nick had divulged that his chequered affair with newscaster Sherry Tate had prompted him to come to England and consider his future in Canada. Sherry travelled the world in her job with Canadian TV and Nick confessed that the relationship had stalled. Reluctant to talk about his problems, Alissa realised that he must have shared his feelings with Erin.

Just as Nick was about to speak again, Max's Land Rover Discovery rumbled into the car park. Max, dressed in a crisp white shirt and a dark tie, climbed out and joined them. After a few minutes' conversation, Nick said goodbye and Max smiled.

'Your brother-in-law is enjoying himself, I take it?' he said in a curious voice as they walked together towards the practice.

Alissa nodded, aware that Max was looking at her. 'Erin rescued him from Kenneth Freshwater. Nick thought the deed deserved, if not a medal, at least a sandwich in the pub. They do seem to get on rather well.'

Max raised an eyebrow. 'You know, it's a mysterious thing,' he murmured as they hesitated at the outer doors, 'this quality we call compatibility. It's invisible and intangible and yet we desperately need it in our lives.'

Alissa looked up at him, surprised at his remark. She had to admit she had often wondered the same herself. 'What would you say the ingredients are that make a couple compatible?' she asked, suddenly intrigued.

His eyes wandered over her face, slowly coming to settle on the soft curve of her open mouth. 'Simple things, I think. Being genuinely interested in one another,' he replied. 'Sharing a physical and emotional attraction - like the song says, someone who, quite literally, takes your breath away.'

Alissa stood still, his words drifting poignantly in the breeze. He remained looking down at her, his gaze unwavering. It took all her will-power to move as she read the unspoken message that was written in his eyes. By the time she managed to pull herself together she was aware that the doors to the surgery had opened and it was time for them to go in.

CHAPTER 10

Two days later, Betty Atkins walked into Alissa's surgery, carrying Sam on her hip. Emily accompanied her mother, displaying her usual lack of interest as Alissa asked her how she was. The little girl merely gazed into space, her plump face surrounded by a mass of curly fair hair.

'Dr Leigh was asking you a question, Emily,' Betty said sharply as she sat down. But Emily made no response and Betty raised her eyes heavenwards. 'She's getting worse. She'll not work up any enthusiasm for anything, then she'll fixate on something silly like an elastic band. Or she'll suddenly get frightened by the sight of an ant crossing the floor. Honestly, you never know what's coming next.' Alissa reached out and grasped Emily's hand, drawing the child gently towards her. 'Why aren't you at school today, Emily? Are you staying at home to help Mummy?' Emily remained silent but Betty explained that her daughter had been sick during the night. It was then that Emily suddenly looked alert and pointed to a mobile that hung from the ceiling. The set of stained-glass cherubs twinkled in the sunlight. 'Pretty lights,' said Emily, fascinated.

'Do you like them?' Alissa turned in her chair to follow the child's gaze.

Emily nodded. 'Sam has lights.'

'She loves strange objects,' Betty said, bouncing Sam on her knee. 'Especially sparkling things. She'll watch the mobiles in Sam's room for hours. Then she'll come and tell me about it, and I'll really think that she is, well ... quite normal. I even think that perhaps she *is* normal though I know that's impossible.'

'It's known as having "islands of normality",' Alissa explained as she watched Emily's face. 'Sometimes a child who is backward in speech can be very clever with mathematics, or have a good, almost photographic memory.' Betty frowned. 'She does sometimes sit with Jamie and scribble.' She added on a deep sigh, 'Not that any of it makes any sense.'

Smiling at Emily, Alissa wrote a few simple sums on a sheet of paper and handed her a pen. 'Show me what you do with Daddy, Emily.'

'I doubt if she will.' Betty shrugged as Emily stared at the paper, then turned it upside down and over in her hands several times.

'You see!' Betty waved her hand dismissively. 'She'll do odd things like that. She'll fiddle with paper for ages. But ask her to do something sensible and you'll wait for ever.'

At this point Sam let out a howl, revealing two pearly white bottom teeth. Betty asked Alissa to examine his sore gums. Emily, seizing her opportunity to disappear, hid behind her mother's chair.

After Alissa had pronounced Sam well, but teething, she brought the subject around to the letter she had sent the Atkinses.

'Jamie hasn't got time to come in,' Betty replied, looking uncomfortable. 'Is Emily's name being put forward to that school or not?'

Alissa hesitated. 'I spoke to my colleagues, but they would like to talk to Jamie first. That's why I wrote to you. For instance, Dr Darvill suggested - '

'You mean, you've discussed this with *him?* Betty interrupted her angrily.

Alissa was astonished at the swift change in attitude. 'I understand Dr Darvill was once Emily's GP and - 'she began, only to be stopped again by Betty.

'It's got nothing to do with anyone else,' Betty snapped. 'I'm Emily's mother. It's my decision. And I don't expect you to go talking about my business behind my back. What you say to your doctor is supposed to be private, isn't it?'

'It is, of course,' Alissa agreed, unable to believe that Betty was reacting in this way.

'Well, I'm not satisfied.' Betty stood up, thrusting Sam onto her hip and glared down at Alissa. 'Being a woman, I thought you'd understand.'

'I can see you want the best for Emily,' Alissa said patiently, 'but there may be other routes to explore closer to home rather than a residential place at a school so far away.'

'Well, I disagree.' Betty squared her shoulders. 'And I should know. The local school is useless.'

'There are other schools,' Alissa suggested, 'and if she was a day pupil, Emily wouldn't need to be taken out of her surroundings - '

'But I told you, neither Jamie nor I have the time to cope with Emily,' Betty cut in, gathering Emily's hand and tugging her towards the door. 'And you're just putting obstacles in the way, as far as I can see. Just like all the rest.'

It suddenly struck Alissa that Betty had already made up her mind about Emily's future and the unpalatable truth was that Betty seemed not to want Emily to remain at home under any circumstances.

Their conversation apparently at an end, Betty marched out, tugging Emily behind her. Confused by her patient's attitude, Alissa reflected that Betty had said something - other than the unpleasant innuendoes she'd made regarding sex and profession - which had caught her attention. Emily often sat with Jamie. That was something Betty had never mentioned before, preferring to imply that Jamie was too busy to give her time.

It was then that Alissa's attention was drawn back to the slip of crumpled paper on the floor. Emily had discarded it as she'd stood behind her mother's chair. Alissa picked it up, unravelled it and studied the large, well- formed numbers.

Emily had completed each sum neatly and without any mistakes.

'I saw Betty Atkins and Emily this morning,' Alissa said that evening as they sat in Max's room, discussing the day's events.

'Not with Jamie, I suppose?' he asked doubtfully as, sitting on the opposite side of the desk, he stretched out his long legs.

'No. Just Emily and Sam.' Alissa paused. 'I'm beginning to wonder if Jamie is aware of what's going on. Perhaps he hasn't even read my letter.'

Max frowned. 'What makes you say that?'

Alissa told him about that morning's conversation and Emily's surprising alacrity with sums. When she described Betty's attitude and the abruptly terminated meeting Max sighed.

'I feared something like this might happen,' he said. 'Did you?' Alissa frowned. 'Why?'

'I had hoped that Betty might have mellowed a little,' he said quietly, 'but obviously not.'

'Do you think Jamie knows anything at all about Betty's intention to send Emily to a residential school?'

Max paused, deep in thought. Then he rose and walked to the window and looked out onto the garden. After a while he turned back, his hands thrust deeply into his trouser pockets. 'I don't know,' he sighed, looking worried, 'but I think it's up to us to find out.'

'It seems I owe you an apology,' Alissa said after a moment's reflection.

'Why is that?'

'I'm not altogether sure that Betty has told me the truth, in fact, I know she hasn't.'

Max nodded slowly. 'Do you want to do as we suggested?'

'You mean call on the Atkinses together?' Alissa shook her head. 'After this morning I don't think turning up at Poplar Farm is going to achieve very much.'

'Then why not ask Annie Partridge to call?'

'Yes, that's probably the best idea,' Alissa decided. 'Annie has given me a brief report but the last time she made a visit to Poplar Farm was just after Sam's birth and she didn't mention whether she saw Jamie or not.'

They were silent for a moment, then he returned to his seat and slowly sat down. 'You'd better know something else, Alissa. Betty wrote an official letter of complaint about me to the local medical authority, saying that my treatment unfairly favoured her husband.' He looked at her from under his dark lashes, distractedly picking up a pen and turning it over several times. 'Jamie wanted a vasectomy. Betty opposed it.'

'A vasectomy?' she repeated incredulously. 'But Betty has given me to understand that Jamie won't consider one.' Max shook his head. 'Jamie came to see me in order to arrange the operation, then cancelled a week later because Betty hit the roof.'

'But I don't understand. Betty has given me a totally different impression.'

Max hesitated as he looked at her. 'I'd hoped I'd never have to mention this, hence the rather abbreviated notes on my part. I didn't want to influence anyone's judgement - I thought it was a matter best forgotten.'

'I see.' Alissa bit her lip, staring down at the desk, the realisation coming to her that Betty's personal life was far from straightforward and that unwittingly she had been drawn into the drama in order to give Betty's argument weight.

'Well, don't let it worry you,' Max said.

She glanced up at him with a rueful smile. 'In the light of what's happened I feel rather foolish,' she admitted, recalling his words at the last practice meeting.

'At this point I'm going to change the subject,' he said with a smile as he leaned forward, resting his arms on the desk. 'Before you slip away, there's something I'd like to ask you.'

She was surprised to see a change of expression in his eyes and involuntarily tensed as his gaze lingered on her face.

'Perhaps you know that this weekend is the Minster Arts Festival,' he said, raising an eyebrow, 'and on Saturday they are having street theatre for the children. I wondered if you'd like to bring Sasha to lunch and then we could join forces for the afternoon?'

'Yes, I know about the festival ...' Alissa hesitated '...but it's Nick's last weekend in England.'

'The invitation is open to Nick, too,' Max said quickly, 'though he told me this morning he's offered to share Saturday morning surgery with Erin. Afterwards I think they're driving out to the New Forest.' Max looked at her with a rueful grin. 'Didn't you know?'

'No, he didn't mention it.' She wondered why but, then, she hadn't had much time to talk to Nick last night as friends had called round and it had been late before they'd left. Nevertheless she was surprised that Erin hadn't mentioned it either.

'In that case I suppose we shall be free,' she acknowledged.

'Fine, we'll leave it at that, then. If Nick's plans change there's no harm done,' he added in a casual tone as they both stood up. 'Nothing that we arrange is ever written in blood as far as I'm concerned.'

It was a pun at which they both smiled as the tension lightened and they went their separate ways. But it was only as she was driving home, her thoughts distracted by the events of the day, that Alissa realised she'd agreed to spend another entire Saturday in Max's company.

CHAPTER 11

ERIN'S LAST PATIENT, Hannah Brent, had been brought straight from school to the surgery by her anxious mother. 'The teacher said she was fine at lunch-time, then this awful rash appeared this afternoon. Whatever is it?'

Erin examined Hannah's chest and saw that the raised white lumps on her skin were surrounded by a nasty inflammation. 'Have you been playing near nettles, Hannah?' Erin asked the little girl.

Hannah looked at her mother and shrugged. 'I might have done.'

'But I've told you never to go near them,' Mrs Brent admonished. 'She knows they sting,' she added, looking crossly at Hannah.

'The rash is called urticaria,' Erin said quickly, giving Hannah a reassuring smile. 'It's an allergic skin rash, usually caused by nettles but not always. Open your mouth, Hannah, please. I just want to have a look inside and check that your mouth is clear from a reaction.'

Hannah opened her mouth and Erin saw that her tongue and throat looked healthy. 'That's fine,' said Erin, sitting back in her chair.

It was evident to Erin the little girl was developing some troubling symptoms of allergic reactions. Erin looked at Mrs Brent who was frowning at her daughter. 'I had hoped to see you at clinic,' she said, and waited until the woman turned to face her.

'I didn't think we needed to trouble you.' Mrs Brent shrugged. 'Hannah seems all right with other foods. It was just the strawberries, that's all.'

'Possibly,' agreed Erin, wondering if Mrs Brent had tried Hannah on the elimination diet. She was about to ask when Mrs Brent spoke again.

'What are you going to give her for this?' She gestured to Hannah's rash. 'It's itching very badly.'

Erin turned to her keyboard and typed in a prescription. 'The rash should go down quite quickly but an antihistamine will help. When you get home give Hannah a cool bath and dab on some calamine afterwards. I would like to see Hannah again in a week's time, as a follow-up appointment at clinic, please.'

Without receiving an assent from the mother, Erin walked with them to her door and said goodbye, wondering what was going through Mrs Brent's mind. Back at her desk she reflected that Hannah had seemed fit enough, other than the rash, so perhaps the reaction to strawberries and nettles were unconnected. However, she'd feel happier when she'd seen Hannah again.

'A penny for them?' someone said, and Erin looked up to find Nick standing at the open door.

She smiled as the colour rushed to her cheeks. 'Oh, they're not worth very much. I'm afraid.' She gestured to the chair. 'Come in, Nick.'

He strode in and sat down, his casual shirt and trousers accentuating his height and thick, dark hair. Since their shared lunch at the Lady Jayne, Erin had wondered if she'd revealed too much about herself during their conversation, but as the minutes had flown by and they'd discussed many different subjects it had felt almost as though she had known him for years rather than days.

Now he was grinning at her and his dark brown eyes held that same disarming expression of appraisal at what he saw.

She smiled, suddenly embarrassed at his scrutiny. 'As a matter of fact, I was thinking about my last patient, a little girl of eight.'

'I thought with that deep frown of concentration you must be thinking of Simon.'

She felt her colour deepen. 'No. I try to keep focused during the day. It's only when I'm at home that I start to brood about the wedding.'

'But why should you brood about it?' he asked, his expression curious as he continued to stare at her.

She didn't know why she had admitted to that and again she felt embarrassed at having spoken her thoughts. 'Oh, last-minute nerves, I think.' She saw he was observing her closely.

'Then I know just the answer,' he said. The next moment he was standing up, coming around to her side of the desk and placing a firm palm under her elbow.

'What do you mean? Where are we going?'

He opened his dark eyes wide. 'To that corner seat at the Lady Jane, of course.'

She tried to protest. She had already agreed to meet him on Saturday afternoon, an arrangement she now regretted. Their drive to the New Forest had been her suggestion, an opportunity for him to see the area, a place which Erin had said she knew well. 'No, Nick, I don't think so,' she said as she realised that, despite his casual manner, he was in earnest as he manoeuvred her towards the door.

'Your surgery is finished isn't it?'

'Yes, but - '

'Doctor's orders,' he told her firmly as he glanced at the heavy gold wristwatch under his white shirt cuff.

'But I can't. I haven't combed my hair or looked at my make-up ...' she flustered.

'You don't need to,' he said as he halted and turned towards her. 'You look lovely as you are. But go and brush up if it makes you feel better. I'll meet you in the car park in ten minutes.'

He disappeared and Erin found herself alone in the room, her heart racing, her legs feeling as though she'd run up and down a steep flight of stairs several times. She felt, well, she wasn't sure what she felt - except she realised that, despite the niggling sensation of disloyalty to Simon should he phone her at home and she wasn't there to answer his call - she was suddenly looking forward to talking to Nick again.

CHAPTER 12

ON SATURDAY MORNING Alissa woke up to bright sunshine creeping through the curtains of her bedroom window. And if she wasn't mistaken, there was the familiar growl of a car engine outside in the drive which meant that Nick was driving in to surgery.

Recalling that he'd had to leave for his eight o'clock surgery with Erin, she pulled on her cotton robe and went downstairs. The kitchen blind was raised and sunshine flooded in across the white worktops and terracotta floor. Nick had carefully washed up his breakfast things and stacked them away in the cupboards. Only the box of cornflakes on the worktop and the aroma of toast was left to reveal his presence in the kitchen.

It was strange, having a man about the house again. Her brother-in-law was so outgoing that despite his problems with Sherry, who hadn't telephoned since his arrival two weeks ago, he had been excellent company.

Staring out of the window, Alissa wondered if Erin had anything to do with it. On Wednesday, after returning home after a drink with Erin at the Lady Jayne, Nick had seemed almost indifferent to Sherry's broken promise to telephone later that night.

Alissa shook her head, reflecting that in two weeks' time Erin would be married and Nick back on the other side of the Atlantic. If there was an attraction between them, it could have little hope of surviving.

Nick was, in any case, involved with Sherry Tate, Alissa reminded herself as she turned back from the window and replaced the cornflakes box in the cupboard. He was reluctant to talk about his long-term affair but Alissa assumed that Nick was still in love with Sherry. Their busy lifestyles were so different, their interests so wildly at odds, that it seemed a strange way to live and love, yet after five years they were, apparently, still involved.

Alissa sighed, turning her thoughts to her own plans for the day. Astrid was staying with friends for the weekend, so it was just breakfast for herself and Sasha. Afterwards, she would enjoy a leisurely coffee as she read the morning paper in the conservatory while Sasha showered and dressed.

She had, she reminded herself as she perched at the breakfast bar, a whole morning to find something suitable to wear, a thought which promptly sent her scurrying upstairs to her wardrobe before Sasha woke up and claimed her full attention.

Sadly, the weather failed to fulfil its early promise. Max rang early and suggested he collect them in the Discovery since he and Bas were out shopping that morning. Their vehicle pulled up in the drive at noon and Sasha ran out to scramble into the back with Bas.

Max waited for Alissa to lock the door and, stopping to buy hot bread from the bakery on their way, they finally ate lunch at Max's house.

After a meal of quiche, salad and the mouth-watering warm bread, it began to drizzle from an unseasonable June sky. To avoid the showers. Max drove them to the town centre and parked, just managing to find a vacant space. By the time they walked to the high street, the canvas tents and stalls were awash with rain.

The place was packed with visitors and the local shops were doing a brisk trade. Dozens of brightly coloured umbrellas jostled for space in the market-place and puddles formed in the gutters. Alissa had worn white cotton pants and a pink waist-tie shirt, but Max, sensibly dressed in jeans and a denim shirt, had brought wet gear. Dressed in these, they were able to tour the streets, dodging the heavier showers.

The street players mimed and performed, heedless of the rain. They braved the elements and collected the coins that came tumbling into their hats. But when thunder grumbled, Max suggested they climb the Minster tower. Ten minutes later and way up high above the bustling streets, they peered down from the ancient turrets.

'It's spooky, Mummy,' whispered Sasha, clinging tightly to Alissa's hand. 'Are there any ghosts here?' 'None,' Alissa assured her. 'And if there were I should think they've all gone inside to keep warm.'

'Mr Gordon says that ghosts aren't real,' announced Bas, eyeing the shadowy corners. 'And 'specially not in daylight.'

Max caught Alissa's eye. 'I think the story goes that all ghosts - if there are any to be found - are usually confined to the west wing.'

Sasha looked up at Max. 'Where's the west wing?'

'Oh, a long way from here,' Max assured her. 'Now, it's starting to rain again, so how would you like to visit the face-painting stall?'

'Yes!' the children squealed, and Max glanced at Alissa, a smile passing between them as Max led the way to the small door at the circular staircase.

As they made their way down the steep steps, Bas was soon out of sight. Sasha hesitated, looking pale. 'I feel funny,' she whimpered. 'My legs have gone all shaky.' Max reached out and lifted her into his arms. 'Hold on tight,' he told her. 'We'll be down in a jiffy.' At the bottom of the staircase he lowered her to the ground and chuckled. 'There, that wasn't too bad, was it?'

Sasha giggled. 'I wasn't really scared. Not really.'

Bas appeared, puffing out his chest. 'Nor was I. Not at all.'

Max grinned and Alissa watched him bend to point the way to the face-painting stall. As the children ran in front of them, he turned to her and held out his hand. She slipped her fingers into his, running with him through the rain.

Sasha looked up with her green cat's face and asked the inevitable. 'Mummy, can Bas stay and play for a while when we get home?'

They were about to leave the face-painting stall and Max, hearing the Minster clock strike five, shook his head. 'Another time, perhaps. It's been a long day for you two.'

'You're welcome to stay for tea.' Alissa looked quickly at Max. 'If you've time, of course.'

'Just a drink will be fine,' he agreed as the two children stared up at them hopefully. 'And after that we must be off.'

When they reached home Bas and Sasha ran upstairs while Max followed Alissa into the kitchen. As she put the kettle on and made drinks for the children she felt nervous, his presence seeming to fill the kitchen as he watched her. She made conversation hardly realising what she was saying until she saw that he was staring through the serving hatch, she had covered the dining room table with a deep red cloth and placed candles next to the long stemmed wineglasses.

'We must go,' he said as his gaze came briefly back to meet hers. 'Don't trouble with coffee. I can see you have a lot to do.'

She was about to reply when the phone rang. She picked up the kitchen extension and heard Nick's voice. He explained that he was eating with Erin and wouldn't be home until late.

'That was Nick,' she told Max seconds later as she replaced the phone, a frown spreading across her forehead. 'He's decided to eat out with Erin.' She glanced ruefully at the table set for two.

Max arched dark eyebrows. 'Your preparations were for Nick?'

She nodded. 'He wasn't to know - it was going to be a surprise. He's not due to leave until Wednesday but I thought Saturday would be a better night to enjoy a leisurely meal as there's no rush to work the following morning.'

Max smiled and she wondered if it had been relief she'd seen fleetingly in his face. 'You must be disappointed after all the trouble you've taken.'

Max was silent and, looking at her with an odd expression, he seemed about to say something more but then thought better of it. 'I'll give Bas a shout,' he said instead, and walked into the hall.

There were, unsurprisingly, cries of protest from upstairs as Max stood at the bottom and looked up, a grin on his face.

'Oh, dear,' sighed Alissa as she came to stand beside him. 'Just when they were enjoying themselves.'

Bas and Sasha came tumbling out of Sasha's room. Bas wore a pair of voluminous crimson pants and Sasha a black leotard.

Max chuckled. 'What's this - fancy dress?'

'We're doing street theatre,' said Bas, 'and making up a play.'

'Bas doesn't have to go yet, does he?' protested Sasha, peering through the banisters. 'Can't Dr Darvill and Bas stay and have some supper with us?'

Alissa looked at Max. 'You're very welcome. As you can see, there's plenty of food. It's a pity to waste it. And,' she added with amusement in her eyes as she glanced at the children, 'it looks as though we may have some entertainment lined up for us this evening.'

It was nine o'clock by the time they'd finished the meal of pasta, fresh vegetables and tuna salad. The children ate banana desserts and Max was tempted to try the selection of cheeses. Bas and Sasha giggled their way through their version of street theatre and, finally exhausted, turned their attention to the computer.

After making coffee, Alissa sat with Max in the conservatory. The rain had stopped but the sky was now dark. Inside it was cosy as they sat together and relaxed in the big armchairs.

Max lowered his coffee-cup to the table, a shadow spreading over his face as he sank back against the cushions. 'Well, I suppose it's time we thought about going.' He looked at her and smiled. 'Not that I want to. But Bas must get some rest. Last night he hardly slept a wink.'

Alissa frowned. 'Was it his asthma?'

Max looked down at his coffee-cup. 'Indirectly. His mother called rather late and it upset him. Punctuality is not one of Priss's finer points. I don't mind for myself, but when it comes to arrangements with the boys I'm afraid I get rather annoyed on their behalf.'

'It must be very difficult for you,' she said into her coffee-cup.

He nodded. 'Particularly for Bas. Aaron is more adjusted to the situation, though he still has his moments.' Alissa remained silent, then said, 'I imagine Aaron has a busy social schedule, like most teenagers have.'

'Yes, which was the underlying cause of all the upset the other week. Priss expressed her disapproval of some of his friends - one girl specifically.'

'Oh,' Alissa remarked, recalling her own teenage angst when it had come to parents' views on boyfriends, 'that's a sensitive subject.'

'It is,' Max agreed darkly, 'but Priss appeared unannounced that day and bumped into Aaron's girlfriend who was waiting in the garden for Aaron to arrive home. It seems that Priss gave the poor girl the third degree, and by the time Aaron got there she was in floods of tears.' Max looked up, his eyes meeting hers. 'I'm afraid I almost lost my temper, but because I know that makes things worse for the boys I tried to make the best of a bad situation.' He shrugged. 'As I said before, I only tolerate such inconsiderateness for their sake.'

Alissa found herself wanting to believe what he was telling her, found herself wanting it so much that she thought she *did* believe him. But hadn't Mike protested in just the same way, insisting that he'd given up his lover and their affair had ceased? In fact, she knew now that Mike had convinced himself - as well as her - that their affair had been over. All to no benefit in the long run, of course. For the heartache had redoubled when she'd discovered Mike had fallen back into his deceptive patterns and that the other woman in his life had still been as real as ever.

Alissa looked at Max, wishing she could believe what he was telling her, but there was that insistent little voice reminding her of the past. And in Max's case the past seemed to be very much a part of the present.

'I don't want to burden you with family problems,' he said quietly as he sat forward, resting his elbows on his knees. 'I really have enjoyed today, though I feel guilty that we ate the meal intended for Nick.'

'I'm glad someone *was* here to eat it,' Alissa replied, glancing up to find that his grey eyes were lingering on her face. He smiled and for a moment there was silence as they gazed at each other. Alissa felt her heart pound as his gaze swept softly over her face and she couldn't miss the look of yearning in his eyes. She didn't resist as he reached out to take her hand, and with a sigh that seemed to come from way down deep inside her she felt herself slide into his arms and lean against his chest.

Max reached up and gently smoothed a stray lock of pale blonde hair from her face, his fingers trailing lightly over her cheek until they came to rest under her chin. He tilted her head until she was gazing directly into his eyes, and what she saw in his expression made her swallow, her lips tingling with anticipation as he moved closer.

'I've wanted to do this for such a long time,' he whispered as his breath fanned her face lightly. 'Today I was imagining, as we stood at the top of the tower, how it would feel to hold you in my arms.'

Then his lips came down and settled gently over hers, a soft enquiry that she responded to until an aching pleasure flooded into every part of her being as she yielded to his embrace and slid her arms around his neck. Closing her eyes, she became lost in another world, one from which she'd been exiled for so long - the taste, sight and touch of a man, this man who aroused in her sensations that were buried so deeply that their release was more shocking to her than she had ever thought possible.

It was then that she heard a noise, far away at first, breaking into her consciousness. Tensing, she realised Max had heard it, too, as he slowly released her mere seconds before the children's voices became audible somewhere in the house.

Alissa moved back to where she had been sitting, smoothing down her skirt. Max stood up and glanced at her briefly, before bending down to pick up his coffee-cup and, in silence, walk with it to the kitchen.

Bas and Sasha had finished with the computer, she realised, and a few minutes later she heard Max's deep voice in the hall, talking and laughing with the children. Standing up and taking a breath, she tried to compose herself, before going out to join them.

CHAPTER 13

ERIN PAUSED as she watched the red Mercedes make its way slowly over the cobbles of the lane and then disappear from view. From where she stood, on the balcony that marked the south-facing wall of her flat, she had a perfect view of the Minster at night.

Little lights twinkled everywhere, the aroma of barbecues mingled with evening scents of grass and the musk of old stone. The Minster, thrown into relief by the pale grey sky with its veins of summer scarlet, stood close by across the market square.

The lights were dim within the ancient building. The smithy's thatch roof obscured the chancel windows, but the foundry's light reflected out into the night. There would still be tourists gazing in at the foundry's window, the last to leave the streets after the day's festival.

She sighed, her mind going back to the long walk she'd taken with Nick that evening. The New Forest had been breathtakingly beautiful and their meal in Salisbury had seemed a perfect end to a lovely day. She had enjoyed Nick's company. And why not? she asked herself as she gazed up at the stars in the sky, a shiver of recollection going over her. Simon had phoned yet again to cancel their plans for the weekend, yet there were only two weeks to go until their wedding. There was so much to discuss ...

Taking one last breath of sweet summer air, Erin went back inside the flat and opened the long window that gave a view of the Minster. She resisted drawing the curtains. The vision of the Minster at night and in the early morning before she left for work was the one thing she would miss when they moved into the cottage. Not that the sale had gone through yet. Simon was dealing with that. It was one of the things she needed to discuss with him as the completion date was the next week. They intended to spend their honeymoon renovating the place. Erin pictured the cottage's timber ceilings and the path leading up to the front door, a path that spilled with wild flowers.Then, unexpectedly, she found herself thinking of Nick. His dark eyes had watched her as she'd told him of her plans for the cottage. They had been walking through fir trees and the smell of pine had been all around them. The scent had seemed intoxicating as it had mingled with the heat of the forest floor. She had stumbled over a root and he had caught her, his hands gripping her with a gentle strength. Glancing up into his dark eyes, there had been a moment between them ... Erin swallowed, felt the heat creep along her hairline. With difficulty she pushed the memory from her mind, just as the telephone rang. With a pang of disappointment she heard her younger sister's voice. Distractedly Erin listened to Kate's enthusiastic chatter about Oxford Street and Covent Garden, but when Kate asked her how she had enjoyed her day, she found herself explaining that Simon hadn't arrived.Unable to bring herself to mention Nick, Erin caught sight of her reflection in the mirror as she talked on the phone. Her eyes were bright and shining and her cheeks were flushed under her chestnut hair. With a spasm of guilt she turned away, looking out onto the Minster, knowing that the woman in the mirror looked far from the disappointed bride-to-be that her sister supposed her to be.

CHAPTER 14

On Monday morning Alissa telephoned Annie Partridge and, thanking her again for her report on the Atkinses, asked her if she had spoken to Jamie yet. The answer was, as Alissa had expected, that she hadn't. Explaining that it had now been agreed that nothing should be done regarding Emily until they were certain of Jamie's views, Annie said that she would telephone the Atkinses and ask to meet them both.

A few minutes later Alissa's first patient arrived. It was with a measure of relief that she recognised Clare Fardon who, smiling anxiously, was standing by the chair at the side of her desk.

'I'm sorry I left like that the last time I saw you,' Clare said immediately. 'I thought I had better come back and apologise.'

'I'm pleased to see you, Clare. I was rather worried.' Alissa gestured to the chair. 'Please, make yourself comfortable.'

Clare hesitated, but finally sat down on the chair. 'I can't stay long. I'm late for school as it is.'

'Have you decided what you want to do?' Alissa didn't want to frighten the girl off again but, despite her agitation, she seemed hesitant to go.

Clare shrugged. 'I haven't seen my boyfriend for a few days now.'

'Perhaps a short break is for the best,' Alissa remarked. 'It might give you time to decide on things.'

Clare nodded, her long fair hair falling over her face. She brushed it back, looking at Alissa from under lowered lids. 'My boyfriend and I want to keep seeing each other, we don't want to split up, but it's difficult. Our families don't really understand. All they think about are exams and study. My father wants me to go to university because he says he always regrets not going himself, even though he likes his job in the police force.

'What about your boyfriend's parents?' Alissa ventured.

'They're divorced,' Clare said at once. 'He lives with his father who - ' Clare stopped abruptly, biting her lip. She blushed and, obviously changing her mind, said quickly, 'His mother doesn't like me very much. She doesn't live around here but she might be moving back, which means we'll have even less of a chance of staying together.'

'And how does your boyfriend feel about all this?' Alissa asked.

Clare shrugged. 'He doesn't want to upset his mother but he's older now, not a kid any more. She doesn't realise that. Nor does his father sometimes. They still treat him like a child.'

'It isn't always easy for parents,' Alissa said consolingly. 'Sometimes children seem to grow up overnight. Adjusting usually takes practice, like everything else worthwhile.'

Clare gave her an old-fashioned look, then lifted her schoolbag into her lap. 'Anyway, I've got to go.' She smiled shyly at Alissa. 'Thanks for the talk. Dr Leigh.'

'That's what I'm here for, Clare.'

Alissa watched the teenager stand up and leave the room. She felt a mixture of sympathy and concern. Sasha would be that age one day. Who knew what problems might befall her? It was a salutary reminder that she herself might be thought of in the same way by her daughter - as a parent who did not understand or sympathise.

Her pretty face hidden beneath her hair, Clare disappeared into the corridor, passing Lyn who was walking along the passageway.

Alissa heard the two speak and seconds later, rather red-faced, Lyn entered the room.

'These young folk,' Lyn sighed, 'always in a rush. I try telling my two boys to slow down but it's like water off a duck's back.'

'How old are they now?' Alissa began to sift through the morning post which Lyn had handed her.

'Ten and fifteen. The ten-year-old's no trouble, but Marcus, the fifteen-year-old, well, he could have a brain on him if he worked harder. All he thinks about is girls and football. I keep on at him - but we seem to fall out when I do. It's a pity because we used to be so close.'

Alissa listened to what Lyn had to say on the subject of her errant son, then returned the pile of inspected post to the receptionist. After Lyn had left the room Alissa sat back thoughtfully, wondering if, when Sasha was older, she herself would be able to tackle teenage problems any more successfully than the average parent. Despite all the experience gained from general practice, and the wealth of information received from patients, she was sensible enough to know that it wouldn't be easy.

As Max had once said, when it came to his own son he wasn't so objective. It was then that Priss Haigh came to mind. Recalling what Clare had said about her boyfriend's mother and father, a note of alarm began to ring in Alissa's head. They were divorced, hadn't she said? The boy was living with his father, the mother was hostile to Clare.

The boyfriend was unwilling to accompany Clare to the surgery. Was he scared of facing up to a frank discussion of contraception or could it be possible that he didn't want to be recognised by anyone there?

Alissa frowned as she wondered if there was a chance that Clare was Aaron's girlfriend. And if that was true, had Max any idea that Priss's intention was to move back to Hayford Minster?

It was a question on which Alissa pondered for the rest of the morning. Still unable to decide whether she was drawing the wrong conclusion or not, she tried to put the matter out of her mind.

After surgery, Max caught up with her in the car park. He called out to her as she was about to unlock her car.

Turning to face him, her heart raced with its now familiar beat of anticipation as he took long strides towards her.

'I phoned you yesterday,' he said breathlessly as he reached her, his eyes searching her face. 'I think you must have been out for the day - I called several times.'

Alissa wished now that she had left the answering machine on as, although she hated to admit it, she had hoped all Sunday evening that the telephone might ring. 'Nick drove us into the country for lunch,' she explained. 'We didn't get back until about five.'

He nodded, his deep tan enhanced by his white shirt and the piercing quality of his silvery grey eyes as he stared down at her. Alissa thought of the moment he'd bent his head and kissed her and the pleasure of leaning against him, her body trembling as she'd inhaled his manly odour - a scent that now blew into her nostrils on the light summer breeze.

'Alissa, when can we meet?' he asked in a voice which sounded suddenly urgent. 'I mean, without the children?'

'That won't be very easy, Max,' she said quietly. 'We must consider the children's feelings.'

'I appreciate that. But we do need to talk. We need a little time for ourselves.'

Though a small part of her had hoped that he would ask her this, she had arrived at no conclusion as to her answer. She was surprised therefore when she found herself answering after only a brief hesitation, 'Well, I'm on call this evening. On Wednesday Nick is leaving ... so that brings us to the end of the week.' She lifted her gaze to his.

'I'm not on call on Friday,' Max said, and, lifting an eyebrow, added, 'Neither are you, I seem to remember.'

'No, but what about the children?'

'It will have to be when they are in bed ...'She nodded hesitantly.

'All right. Friday, then.' He smiled at her, giving her the same intimate glance that made her feel like a teenager again, but save for a brisk goodnight they said no more. Alissa watched him hurry to the Discovery and drive away, a little cloud of dust spinning up from the back wheels as the big vehicle left the car park. She took a deep breath, expelled it slowly and when she felt calmer finally started her own car.

CHAPTER 15

THE WEEK PASSED SWIFTLY, marked by Alec Rogers's return to work and Nick's departure on Wednesday evening. The fact that Nick had seemed reluctant to leave England surprised Alissa for his next stop was in Brussels and a rendezvous with Sherry. As she and Sasha waved goodbye, she was left with the feeling that her brother-in-law was in no great haste to see his long-time love.

On Friday, however, Nick sent a fax and all seemed well as he wrote that he and Sherry were making a trip to Italy, before returning to Canada.

Alissa hurried home from surgery at five-thirty that day. She drove past the travellers' campsite, wondering if she might catch sight of India or Sky. The small circle of caravans was still there but she saw no sign of the young travellers or the baby. The hospital had sent her a report stating that Orion's operation had been successful, the child discharged and given an appointment for Outpatients. Perhaps Sky had returned and all was now well with the family, she decided. As she headed towards home and the prospect of the hours ahead, a faint thrill of excitement went through her at the thought of her evening visitor.

On reaching Green Gables, she found Astrid and Sasha sitting in the conservatory. Sasha's chin was cupped in her hands. 'I'm listening to Astrid's verbs,' she declared in a grown-up fashion as Astrid balanced a book in front of her on her knees.

Alissa dropped her bag on the floor and sank into one of the rattan chairs. Pleased with her audience, Astrid reeled off her verbs until Alissa, only half concentrating, suggested it was time for supper. Alissa had little appetite as she prepared a meal. Max had arranged to call at nine o'clock and she wanted to have Sasha settled by then. Fortunately Astrid was going out that evening to play squash with her friends, and by half past eight they had eaten and cleared away and Sasha was in bed. She was tired from her swimming lesson at school and soon she was asleep, tucked snugly under the covers. Alissa always left on a night-light and she closed the bedroom door softly, standing outside it for a moment to listen. Finding herself dithering over what to wear, Alissa selected a sarong-style skirt and turquoise silk blouse, knowing she had only a short time to change. The blue complemented her darker blue eyes and her freshly washed blonde hair and the skirt made her feel cool and feminine. Trying to offset the butterflies in her stomach, she plumped up the cushions in the drawing-room where she intended to sit with Max. Several times she glanced out of the window, wondering if Sasha would wake when she heard the sound of the vehicle. But when the Discovery finally pulled into the drive all remained quiet upstairs and Alissa opened the front door to greet him.

'Sorry I'm late,' he apologised at once, looking as though he, too, had hurried, his shower-damp hair falling over his face. 'Bas has only just gone to bed and Aaron was late coming home.' He wore an ivory linen shirt and light-coloured chinos and his grey eyes were uncertain as he hovered on the doorstep. 'Is Sasha in bed?'

She nodded and gestured for him to enter, the nervous feeling in her stomach beginning to escalate into a certainty that this meeting was going to be an embarrassing mistake. What if, without the children, they had little to say to one another? Or they decided that neither of them were prepared for this moment?

Her eyes must have shown her doubts as he glanced over her

shoulder, a frown creasing his forehead. 'Are you sure this is convenient?'

She realised then that they were both anxious and she held out her hand, the gesture causing him to smile, the muscles in his face immediately relaxing. He slid his fingers around hers and stepped towards her as she closed the door.

'I'm glad you're here,' she whispered, and in the silence that followed he bent to kiss her mouth.

After a few seconds they walked together to the large room on the right and once again Alissa closed the door, listening for a few seconds before turning to him.

He pulled her close, and this time his embrace left her in no doubt as to the reason for his visit, the chemistry between them undeniable. He drew a ragged breath and sighed unevenly. 'Alissa ...'

Her arms were linked behind his neck, her skin shivering at the feel of his body against hers. 'You know, since Mike died I haven't dated,' she whispered, and he smiled, taking her face between his hands.

'It's been the same for me. The occasional night at the theatre or perhaps dinner with a friend. But nothing more.'

She nodded, desperate to dispel any awkwardness that might arise between them. She spoke in a rush. 'Would you like a drink? I've some chilled wine, or coffee, or perhaps tea?'

He didn't answer, but lowered his mouth over hers in a kiss that was long and searching. To her utter joy she found her doubts evaporating as she slid her arms around his neck again, inhaling the tangy scent that made her heart flutter with indescribable pleasure. Her lips parted willingly to respond to the pressure of his kiss, acknowledging the mutual longing that had brought them together this evening.

How long they remained in each other's arms she didn't know, but he finally lifted his head and, catching a long breath, looked into her eyes. *I had no idea how you would feel,* ' he said so softly she could barely hear him. 'I wondered if I'd imagined this. I almost expected you to ask me why I was here.'

Her fingers lay lightly on his shoulders, gripping the strong bone and muscle that flexed briefly beneath her touch. She shook her head, smiling. 'I wondered if you would come, and if we were doing the right thing - even wondered if we would have much to say to one another without the children.'

'I think we've soon answered that,' he said, and grinned. 'I couldn't wait to get here. We never seem to have a moment to ourselves -'

'We didn't need one - once,' she interrupted, and laughed softly.

He nodded, a rueful smile touching his lips. 'So, Dr Leigh, do you mind telling me what you think has changed?'

She looked into his eyes and lifted her shoulders on a sigh. 'I don't know, except that we are both ...'

'Attracted to one another?' He lowered his head and kissed her softly, his lips searching for her response. When she gave it his arms tightened around her and there seemed no need for words. But as they broke apart his voice was husky with need as he said, 'The question is, where do we go from here?'

She looked at him, her gaze steady. 'Where do you want us to go, Max?'

'I want to see more of you. I want to be with you.' His answer was simple and she wanted - needed - to believe him because that was how she felt, too. But did he really mean what he said, or was she merely listening to the words of a man who was struggling to be free from the emotional ties of another woman, a woman whom he had loved and who had given him his sons? A woman like Priss, powerful and possessive, a woman who would never relinquish what she deemed hers.

Alissa pushed herself back from him, the thought making her cold inside. Freeing herself from his arms, she turned to the table where she had set out some drinks.

Through the brick-fringed arches of the big room it was possible, even at dusk, to see out onto the woodland that bordered her garden. A high red-brick wall covered in wisteria circled the soft green lawns that ran down to the terrace. The room tended to be light and, filled with fragrant plants, its vast spaces were always aromatic. The long, L-shaped cushion-filled sofa and rattan armchairs gave the place a subdued quality and she was grateful for its tranquillity as she filled two glasses with wine.

Max also stood, looking out at the view, and for a moment she watched him, her breathing shallow as the silence deepened around them. She lifted the glasses and handed him one. He took it silently, his gaze lowering to her eyes.

'Let's sit down,' she said quietly and he smiled, walking beside her to the big sofa. As she sat down beside him his gaze went towards the white-painted dresser in the corner. 'Your husband?' he said quietly.

She nodded, glancing at the photo of Sasha in her father's arms. 'Sasha was two then. Mike and I were in practice together in Kent.' Alissa paused. 'It was taken fifteen months before the crash.'

'It must have been terrible for you,' Max said quietly. He looked at her with sympathy in his eyes.

'We had just moved to Hayford Minster. Mike had been away for the weekend, and was on his way home when it happened. A lorry jackknifed on the motorway. Mike was behind it and was killed outright.'

'Had you known each other long?' he asked after a while.

'We met while I was training. He was a GP in Kent - I knew his secretary, Fiona Carey. She introduced us at a party. Nine months later we were married. I joined Mike in practice and three years later Sasha was born.' There was silence for a moment as she hesitated, the memories of her marriage to Mike flooding back - one in particular of the day she'd returned to the surgery unexpectedly. She had wondered since if she would ever forget the sight of the two figures as she'd opened the door - Mike and Fiona in each other's arms, the shocked looks on their faces when they'd seen her standing there.

She glanced down at the glass in her hands. 'Alec Rogers was a friend of Mike's,' she went on. 'He suggested a partnership between the three of us. We agreed - we felt we needed a new challenge.'

'Yes, I remember you joining Alec.' Max paused. 'Though I didn't ever have a chance to meet your husband, Alec told me a lot about you both.' He reached out to slide his fingers under her chin and lift it. He looked into her eyes and as she swallowed her eyes became misty.

She didn't resist as he took her untasted drink and placed it, together with his, on a low table. Leaning back, he drew her into his arms, pressing her head against his chest. After all this time, she wondered, how could Mike's betrayal still hurt so much?

'I'm sorry,' she apologised. 'This is ridiculous.'

'No, it isn't,' he told her gently. 'It's perfectly natural.'

'I didn't realise talking about it would still upset me,' she admitted, though she couldn't bring herself to explain about Fiona.

'There's no time limit on grief,' he said softly. 'We see it in our work every day. You mustn't be so hard on yourself.'

Was it still grief that shadowed her life? she wondered. She had tried to put the past behind her, avoiding confronting the painful memories associated with her marriage and Mike's sudden death. The tragedy was that their move to Hayford Minster had been as a direct result of their efforts to try to save their relationship, an effort which had ended in Mike returning to see Fiona that weekend.

Suddenly Max bent his head to kiss her and his lips took away the memory of anything else but that moment. Her body trembled against him as she wanted to answer that she, too, yearned to be made love to. Mike had been her only love. After he'd died, despite the circumstances which had led to his death, she had wanted no other man. Since then her only concern had been to give Sasha the love and security she so desperately needed.

But now her body was urgent with need and she refused to contemplate what lay ahead. As if they had both drawn the same conclusion, she didn't move as his kiss deepened and his fingers dropped to caress the smooth curve of her breast. A thrill went through her and she felt desire burn inside her, too great this time to be ignored.

'I want you, Alissa. You know that, don't you?' he whispered against her lips.

She nodded, swallowing. 'Yes, I know.'

He pulled her closer, his mouth finding hers again, their passion devouring them. For a wild moment she let all other thoughts go as his arms encircled her, but then the real world drifted back and she thought of Sasha sleeping upstairs and the years of striving to restore her confidence after the accident.

'Sasha should sleep,' she said softly, 'but I don't want to risk her coming down here.'

He nodded slowly, his fingers running softly over her skin.

'I know. I understand.'

She watched her fingers as if in a dream as they lay on his shirt and she lifted them to caress the tanned skin above his collar where tiny sinews quivered against her touch.

Only the light from the lamp played on them as her eyes closed and he slid soft kisses down the curve of her neck. The passion she had stored up was overflowing and, drawing the same intensity from him, there was no mistaking the desire in his eyes.

'I'd better go,' he said quietly, 'because if I stay ...' His voice tailed off and she understood what he meant.

They rose unsteadily and in the silence he bent to kiss her for the last time. His lips were warm and sweet and she arched against him, her hips curved against his body, a hunger, intense and deep, welling up inside her.

'Alissa,' he moaned softly as he hugged her to him.

Overwhelmed by the need that filled her, she sighed, the pent up desires and longings of the past three years suddenly released into the anguished groan that came from her throat.

'It's all right,' he whispered against her cheek. 'It's all right.'

She felt that he understood. She felt she had known him for ever, that their thoughts seemed to connect and that, even if it had been possible for them to have made love tonight, no moment could have been sweeter than this.

She wanted with all her heart to give in to it, to let go, to allow the frustration and anguish of the lonely years to simply drain away as she satisfied this urgent hunger. Her body shuddered and he kissed her again, taking in a brief, ragged breath.

Gently, he moved away from her and silently opened the door. She followed him into the hall. She was beside him in a few seconds and, turning the key in the lock, she opened the front door.

'You look lovely in the moonlight, do you know that?' he said, lifting his hand to her hair. He bent his head and kissed her with a restrained energy. 'I think we have to make time for ourselves. And, I promise you, we will.' He threaded his fingers through her hair, tucking its silky waves behind her ears. 'I don't want to go, but I must.'

She stood very still, barely breathing. His eyes were full of yearning which had been suddenly tempered, and she sighed, knowing that whatever it was she wanted to say would not leave her lips.

'Tonight was wonderful,' he said quietly, before stepping out into darkness. She watched his figure move silently down the path and finally she heard the sound of the Discovery's engine. Waiting until she knew he was gone, she closed the door and leaned heavily back against it.

CHAPTER 16

WHEN ASTRID RETURNED home Max was long gone.

'Did you have a nice evening?' she asked in her broken English. Alissa walked through from the kitchen in her cotton dressing-gown, carrying a glass of milk.'

Yes, and you?' Alissa replied hesitantly, self-conscious about her unsteady hands and flushed face. Seeming not to notice, Astrid made her way to bed and Alissa sat downstairs in the drawing-room to drink her milk, allowing herself to relax for the first time that evening. Her mind travelled back over what had happened and she wondered if Max had really been serious about sharing time with each other. It would be difficult with the children to consider but, despite that, Alissa still trembled at the thought of his body close to hers. With this thought came another. Could there possibly be a future for them or would the physical gratification they both seemed to need so much die after a brief affair?

And, of course, there was Priss. It was difficult to imagine that Max would ever be free of her, especially if it was true that she intended to move back from Paris to Hayford Minster. Could she really allow herself to be exposed to the same kind of risk she had taken with Fiona Carey?

Alissa sighed at the memory of her dead husband's mistress. Beautiful and self-willed, like Priss, Fiona Carey had never been far from Mike's thoughts. Was Priss in Max's thoughts, too? Did he simply use the boys as an excuse?

Alissa rose and went to the kitchen to rinse out her glass. Even if she knew the answers to those questions, it would be difficult to find time for a man in her life. So was that what she really wanted? Had she thought an affair through? And there was something else that she hadn't given a thought to - their professional relationship. Wasn't it a risk to become emotionally involved when there was so much at stake?

It was as she climbed between the sheets that she smelt Max's faint scent on her hair. She turned her head into it as she lay on the pillow and imagined him lying beside her. Was there a place for him in her life, or in his life for her? she asked herself. Or would this night, after sensible reflection, best be forgotten?

CHAPTER 17

ALISSA WAITED all weekend for the telephone to ring, but Max didn't call. The only person to ring, late on Sunday afternoon, was Erin.

'I've a favour to ask,' she said hesitantly. 'Could you possibly fit one more in your car next Saturday?'

Alissa had to stop to think for a moment, then realised she had been so preoccupied with her own thoughts that she had forgotten the wedding. 'Of course,' she agreed at once. 'Who is it?'

'It's Kirstie, our practice manager. She won't have the car that weekend. Her husband's away in Scotland. As you know, Kirstie lives out of town.'

'No problem,' said Alissa. 'I'm driving Sasha to her friend's house for the weekend. I'll collect Kirstie afterwards.'

'Are you sure it won't be too much?' Erin asked.

'Not at all,' Alissa assured her. 'I'll ring and confirm with Kirstie now.'

On the day of the wedding Sasha was going to stay with a friend from school. It was Amy Lewis's birthday and Caroline, Amy's mother, had suggested that Sasha stay for the night. Alissa had given Sasha the choice of going to Erin's wedding or accepting her friend's invitation and Sasha had decided to accept Amy's invitation. So, Alissa reminded herself, while she was looking for a gift for Erin and Simon, she must also remember to buy something for Amy.

Alissa rang Caroline and confirmed the arrangement, then rang Kirstie who accepted the offer of a lift. Still Max didn't telephone.

On Monday, when Alissa arrived at the surgery, she found that Hannah Brent had been slotted in as an emergency patient.

'She's been sneezing and coughing all weekend,' her mother explained. 'Her eyes have been itching and she's rubbed them raw.'

'Have you tried the antihistamine that was prescribed for Hannah's allergy?' Alissa asked as she studied Hannah's notes.

'I don't believe she does have an allergy,' Mrs Brent retorted. 'Hannah is a healthy child.'

Alissa examined the little girl. Although the sneezing and itching had ceased, she had been left with a chest infection.

'It sounds a little noisy down there,' Alissa said as she put away her stethoscope and smiled at Hannah. 'We'll give you something to help clear the passageways.' She looked at Mrs Brent. 'Is Hannah able to take penicillin?'

'I think so,' replied the woman vaguely. 'Is penicillin really necessary?'

'In this instance, yes.' Alissa prescribed a suitable antibiotic and printed out the prescription, handing it to Mrs Brent. 'Plenty of rest and lots of fluid to drink. I'd like to see her again after she's finished the course.'

'We usually see Dr Brooks ...' Mrs Brent frowned at the prescription and for a moment Alissa wondered if she might be about to hand it back. 'But she was fully booked this morning.'

'Dr Brooks has two weeks' leave as from Friday,' Alissa explained as Hannah's mother folded the prescription and put it into her bag. 'But I'll be happy to see Hannah next week.'

Mrs Brent rose and took hold of Hannah's hand. 'I really don't like her taking these drugs. You never know what's in them or what side effects they have, especially on a child of eight.'

Before Alissa could respond, Hannah had been led away. Alissa stared thoughtfully at the open door of her consulting room, confused at the woman's attitude. On the one hand she wanted attention for Hannah, but on the other she maintained her daughter was well and needed no medication. However, as Hannah was Erin's patient, she would leave Erin to unravel the mystery. It was much later in the day when she heard Max's voice outside her door. He spoke to Lyn, his deep voice unmistakable in the corridor, then he knocked. Alissa called out for him to enter, and as he did so her heart leapt as he smiled his familiar crooked smile.

After closing the door behind him, he strode across the room and took her in his arms, kissing her fully on the mouth. Then, looking into her eyes, he shook his head, slowly releasing his grip as he sighed. 'I just don't seem to be able to keep a sensible head around you. And this weekend seemed such a long one.'

'Yes, it did,' she whispered as he seemed unable to decide whether to release her. Finally they drew apart and Alissa sat down, her heart beginning the ridiculous accelerated beat of anticipation which she was now becoming accustomed to when he touched her.

'It's been chaotic at the house, I'm afraid.' He sat down heavily on the chair beside her desk. 'I intended to phone you, but every time I picked the damn thing up some crisis erupted.' He thrust a hand through his dark hair. 'Aaron decided to bring his girlfriend home. She's a pleasant enough youngster, but they wanted to go away for the weekend, camping - alone. I refused and explained I had no objection to them going in a group under supervision, but that idea fell flat, as you can imagine. They hung around the house for most of the time, hoping to wear me down, until eventually Clare left.'

'Clare?' repeated Alissa, at once alert.

'Clare Fardon.' Max paused. 'Her father is a policeman - I doubt he would have thought much of the camping idea either.'

If she admitted she knew the girl he would expect her to comment, so in view of what she knew of Aaron's and Clare's relationship she said nothing. There was nothing she could do or say to help, she realised, and for a moment she looked away from Max's perceptive stare.

Leaning forward, he reached out to take her hand. 'I missed you,' he whispered softly, 'very much.'

They looked at each other for a while and then he rose, came around the desk and pulled her to her feet. 'Damn it,' he whispered huskily, 'I can't resist you.' He kissed her, his lips warm and hungry over hers.

Very soon the sound of footsteps came through the door and they pulled apart quickly.

'Dr Darvill?' Lyn called outside. 'Your next patient is waiting.'

He lifted his shoulders in a heavy shrug. 'Better go,' he said, a regretful smile on his lips. 'See you later? Perhaps we can snatch some time together soon.'

Alissa nodded, but she didn't know where or when and at that moment she hadn't the courage to ask.

CHAPTER 18

ON WEDNESDAY ALEC informed Alissa that he had seen Betty Atkins and had given her an antenatal check. Alissa was again bewildered by Betty's attitude. She could only assume that Betty didn't want to be tackled about Jamie and had booked in with Alec instead.

Since Annie Partridge had failed to find Jamie at the farm, Alissa resolved to wait until Betty approached her. If she still wanted Emily to have a place at the residential centre then she must at some point pursue the matter.

That night Alissa gave a small party for Erin. The girls from the surgery came, as did Erin's friends and her two sisters, Kate and Patti. They had an evening of fun and laughter, tempered by the fact that Simon hadn't telephoned to confirm his arrival the following day. Earlier in the week he had admitted to having a cold and Erin was concerned about his health. Max phoned after the party was over. 'By the sound of it, you had a good time,' he remarked dryly.

'It was fairly civilised for a hen night,' Alissa admitted. 'How about you? Are the boys OK?'

'Yes, they're fine ...' She heard his indrawn breath. 'You know. I've been thinking about Saturday,' he said, and paused again. 'I thought perhaps, after the reception, we could slip away without too much difficulty. There's a hotel that's always taken my eye on the way to Salisbury. What do you say to the idea we try to arrange sitters for the children over the weekend?'

Alissa felt a thrill go through her. 'That sounds wonderful, Max.'

'Shall we settle on it, then?'

'Why not?' she murmured, thinking that Sasha's weekend was already taken care of. 'Can you find someone to stay with Bas?'

'Mrs Dunphy,' he said at once. 'She'll be quite happy to stay the night. What about Sasha?'

'She's staying with a friend, as it happens,' she said, hardly able to believe that they were both really going to spend time together without the children. She went to bed feeling ridiculously like a moonstruck sixteen-year-old. She lay awake for hours, unable to sleep, thinking of the weekend ahead of her. She could hardly believe how happy she felt - and yet should she really allow herself to feel this way? Where was this relationship going? she wondered. And what did the future hold? Was she being utterly foolish in believing that Max could ever share his life with her? In the light of what Clare Fardon had said, would Priss return to live in Hayford Minster and was it hopelessly naive of her to think that Max could ever free himself from her hold?

Alissa realised that she was approaching the stage where she wouldn't actually listen to reason. Despite the fact that Max had assured her that he only tolerated Priss in his life for the boys' sake, she was still filled with doubt.

One decision, however, had now been made. The weekend ahead meant that she would spend two whole days and one night in Max's company. Whatever her doubts, she had agreed to that much.

Finally on the brink of sleep, Alissa heard her bedroom door open.

'Mummy?' Alissa sat up and turned on the bedside light.

'Darling, what is it?'

'I've got a snuffly nose.'

Alissa threw back the sheets and drew Sasha into bed beside her.

'Have all the ladies gone?' Sasha asked as she snuggled up.

'All gone, darling.'

'You were laughing a lot.'

'Did we disturb you?'

'No. It was nice. I like a lot of people here. I like it best when Dr Darvill and Bas come over. All my friends have brothers ...' Sasha paused and Alissa wondered what was coming next. 'And lots of them have daddies, too,' Sasha added sleepily.

Alissa sighed and kissed her daughter's hot forehead. An ache in her heart for Sasha caused her to catch her breath as she wrapped her arms about her daughter. The family she had always wanted with Mike had never materialised, despite their efforts, and for some time now she had reconciled herself to the fact that Sasha would be her only child.

Sasha sneezed. A summer cold - that's all we need, Alissa thought as Sasha sniffed and she was forced to struggle out of bed to find a box of tissues, the subject of brothers thankfully forgotten.

Sasha didn't go to school the following day. She didn't have a cold but she was tired and, bearing in mind that she was going away for the weekend, Alissa thought it wiser to keep her home.

On Friday, Sasha was up early and seemed fit. Alissa offered to drive her to school but Sasha had other ideas. 'If we're early Astrid takes me to the park,' she announced, scooping the last of her cornflakes from her bowl. 'There's a new slide there that's really slippery.'

So, with time to spare, Alissa drove the long way to work, intending to pass Hayford Minster Wood. She had seen nothing more of India and Orion and wondered if the caravans had moved on.

On the top of Hayford Hill, a local beauty spot, a bright flash of what looked like a windscreen reflecting sunlight in the dip below momentarily blinded her. It disappeared again as she descended and the road levelled out. She expected to see another vehicle pass her, but nothing did.

Driving around the bend, she noticed half a dozen saplings snapped off from their trunks, lying at the side of the road. The splintered wood was fresh and Alissa was curious to know what had happened. She parked her car on the grass verge and got out to take a closer look.

DOCTOR DON'T LEAVE

At that moment a vehicle's horn sounded. A green Discovery swerved in beside her, throwing a wave of dust up from its back wheels. Alissa remembered that Max was on call this morning and that he must have been on a visit.

'Are you all right?' he called, hurrying over to her. 'Have you broken down?'

'I'm fine,' she assured him, 'but I saw a flash of light from the top of the hill. It was rather odd. I didn't pass another vehicle on my way down and then I saw those trees.' She pointed to the trail of broken saplings.

They walked together to the verge, following the fresh skid marks which had churned up the grass. 'You're right - there's a car down there,' he murmured as, going closer to the edge, they both peered down the slope.

'It's a taxi, isn't it, from the sign on the roof?'

'I'll get my case from the car,' Max said hurriedly. Alissa did the same and, meeting again at the verge, they scrambled down together. The driver's door was open and from the rear of the taxi, a white face peered out. Max hurried around to the side that was clear of obstruction. 'It's all right, I'm a doctor,' Alissa heard him say as he opened the door and climbed in.

As she waited, she looked around. There was no sign of anyone else and the briar and bramble made it impossible to go deeper into the wood. After a while Max emerged, dragging his case after him. 'The woman tells me her name is Mrs Bowen,' he explained hurriedly. 'She was travelling to London to catch an early morning flight from Heathrow. She intended to travel to the USA to visit her daughter. The taxi collected her at five o'clock in the morning and the accident happened soon afterwards, which means she's been stuck down here for almost four hours.'

'What are her injuries?' Alissa asked. 'Are they serious?'

'As far as I can detect, she has a painful posterior hip dislocation. I've administered an analgesic, but she needs swift hospital attention. I'm also concerned for the driver. He left the car to get help but hasn't returned. I ought to take a look around after I've phoned the emergency services.'

'While you do that,' suggested Alissa, ducking down to look into the car, 'I'll see to Mrs Bowen.'

Max nodded, then climbed the slope again. Meanwhile, Alissa did what she could for the elderly woman, immobilising her injured leg by securing it to the other one with the use of padding and triangular bandages. By the time the police and ambulance arrived the analgesic had begun to take affect, and the paramedics were able to transfer her, fairly painlessly, to a stretcher.

Alissa scrambled up the slope beside the small convoy, then joined Max by the cars. He was in conversation with a policeman. Their one clue to the driver was a dark-coloured jacket which Max had found on the road.

At that point Max's pager sounded and he was called away to a visit. The police kept her only a few minutes more but the accident had delayed her considerably. She abandoned the idea of Hayford Minster Wood and flew back over the hill, arriving three quarters of an hour late for surgery.

'Dr Leigh, I'm afraid you're on your own for a bit.' Lyn announced as Alisa walked in. 'It's panic stations this morning.'

'Isn't Dr Rogers here yet?'

Lyn shook her head. 'And Mo has broken down in her car. She said she'll be here as soon as the repairman has fixed it.'

Alissa sighed, peeling off her jacket as she walked across the room to the reception desk.

'How many are waiting?'

Lyn grimaced. 'Three of yours, two of Dr Rogers's. Oh, and to add to your problems, there's someone in the recovery room. He isn't a patient - or at least he might be but we aren't sure. I think you'll find he needs stitches in a head wound.'

'Have you checked his name and date of birth on the database?' Alissa asked, wondering why the casualty hadn't taken himself to hospital.

Lyn frowned. 'That's just the trouble - we don't know his name. He either won't or can't give it to us. As he looked pretty groggy, all I could think of doing was putting him in the recovery room for now.'

'All right,' Alissa sighed, surrendering herself to what threatened to be a fraught Friday. 'Tell everyone I'm running late, but if they're prepared to wait I'll see them as soon as I can.'

Once in her room Alissa dropped her coat and bag onto her chair, ignored the pile of post on her desk and hurried to the recovery room. The man was sitting on the hard chair by the examination bench. He was about forty, she gauged, with untidy dark hair flecked with grey. His shirt was dirty and so were his trousers, and he held a handkerchief to his head.

'Good morning,' she said as she stepped forward to remove the handkerchief. A deep cut stretched from hairline to temple. 'That looks like a nasty wound. How did you do it?'

He shook his head and shrugged. 'I don't know,' he responded vaguely. 'I can't remember a thing.'

'Can you tell me your name or how you got here?'

He shook his head again. 'No ... I don't remember.' He patted his empty trouser pockets. 'I don't appear to have a wallet either but I seem to think I had a coat ... and I've this bump on my head.'

He was, decided Alissa, suffering from concussion at the very least. As she examined his wounds and saw the extent of bruising, she became convinced the man was the driver of the taxi. Perhaps he hadn't been wearing his seat belt and had sustained his injuries as the car had hurtled off the road.

Asking Lyn to phone the police, Alissa meanwhile cleaned and sutured the man's wounds. By the time she'd finished the neat row of stitching, a uniformed policeman had arrived.

'We'll take him to Casualty,' the officer told Alissa, as nothing more could be added to the information she had given them. 'Mrs Bowen might be able to identify him and we'll go from there.'

Now an hour late for her patients, Alissa hurried back to her room. Just as she was about to enter, Alec limped into the corridor. He wore a sling on his right arm and he was obviously walking with pain.

'Alec! Whatever has happened?'

He shuffled slowly towards her, raising his bushy grey eyebrows. 'I fell down the stairs during the night. The damn light-bulb in the hall had burst and I couldn't see a thing. I managed to fracture my wrist and sprain my ankle.'

'Oh, Alec, I'm sorry,' Alissa said sympathetically. 'You shouldn't be here. Why don't you go home and rest?'

Alec laughed. 'I'll manage somehow. They say trouble comes in threes. I may as well be here to witness the third.'

Just then a movement behind her caused her to turn sharply. 'Has anyone seen Max?' demanded a familiar female voice.

Trouble number three had arrived, it appeared, though not in the way either she or Alec had anticipated, Alissa thought with a sigh. Priss Haigh was hurrying down the corridor towards them.

CHAPTER 19

It was a quarter to seven that evening when Alissa finally emerged from her surgery. Ruth and Keeley, the evening staff, were busy clearing up the play area. The allergy clinic was over, but the trail of toys and books left by the children were yet to be restored to their shelves.

'Whew!' sighed Keeley, approaching Alissa with an armful of magazines. 'What a day!'

Alissa nodded, blinking away the tiredness from her eyes. She pushed her blonde hair from her forehead and took some of the magazines from Keeley's arms. 'Here, let me help.'

Keeley protested. 'No, I'll manage. Dr Leigh. You look all in.'

Alissa smiled and, ignoring Keeley's offer, tucked the magazines onto the shelves.

Soon they had the area tidy and, joining Ruth at the desk, Alissa paused to ask how Alec had coped with his surgery.

'With difficulty,' Ruth said with a sigh. 'But he coped. I suppose you know Dr Darvill was delayed?'

Alissa shook her head. 'What happened?'

'The moment he got back from his calls,' Ruth said, unable to hide her disapproval, 'his wife - sorry, ex-wife - pounced on him. I happened to be standing there and couldn't help overhearing. Well, it's not up to me to comment but I think it's common knowledge that Dr Darvill only goes along with her for the sake of his boys.'

Alissa saw Keeley's expression, which denoted that she was in complete agreement with her friend. However, Alissa merely nodded and then changed the subject to the lists for Monday morning.

By seven o'clock she had finished her correspondence and, gathering her things, she walked out to Reception, calling goodnight to Ruth.

'Oh, by the way. Dr Leigh ...' Ruth held up her hand. 'I almost forgot to give you a message from Dr Darvill. He asked me to tell you he wouldn't be able to go to the wedding tomorrow and -' The telephone rang and Ruth sighed again. 'Sorry, I'll have to take it - Keeley's gone home.' Ruth lifted the receiver and was soon deep in conversation.

Alissa didn't wait for her to finish. She hurried out to the car where she sat behind the steering-wheel, tears at the corners of her eyes. Why hadn't Max stopped to tell her about tomorrow? She had been so looking forward it. How could he let her down like this?

The ache of disappointment filled her again, as it had during her marriage to Mike. She took a tissue and blew her nose. Despite Ruth's remark that Max only went along with Priss for the sake of the boys, nothing could allay Alissa's fears. Finally starting the car, she drove out of the car park and headed for home.

CHAPTER 20

ALISSA SLID on her new dress, a calf-length, pale blue silk creation she had bought for the wedding. The mirror told her she looked perfect. The dress fitted her slender figure as though it had been hand-made for her. The material was soft and smooth and was the same shade of deep turquoise as her eyes. Her hair had fallen into place with ease, soft blonde waves spilling around her face and accentuating her features.

After yesterday's news that Max wouldn't be able to attend the wedding her excitement had drained away and she knew that her heart wouldn't be in the celebrations.

'Mummy, it's late!' Sasha bounded into the room. 'Amy will think I'm not coming.'

'We've five minutes to spare,' Alissa assured her, and with a sigh picked up the white leather handbag she had bought to go with the dress.

'Have we got Amy's present and card?' Sasha asked as she stared at her mother, her eyes going over the blue dress.

Alissa gestured to the gift lying on the bed. 'Yes. It's wrapped and ready for her.'

She had bought a set of water-colour paints after her visit to the boutique, and had also chosen a set of crystal glasses for Simon and Erin.

Sasha frowned. 'You look pretty. Will Dr Darvill be there?'

Alissa shook her head. 'No, he won't.'

'Oh,' remarked Sasha, obviously disappointed. 'Anyway, you still look pretty.'

Alissa walked over and bent to hug her daughter. 'Thank you, darling, that makes all the effort worthwhile.'

Alissa watched Sasha skip off, then turned her thoughts towards the wedding. It was a special day and long awaited by Erin. She glanced around her and mentally checked off the things she had to take with her. Keeping her mind focused, it would help to offset her own disappointment. Suppressing a sigh, she sat down at her dressing-table to add the last touches to her make-up.

After dropping Sasha at Amy's and calling for Kirstie, Alissa took her place in the church and sat quietly after the early morning rush. The Minster was full of gorgeous flowers and there was a pleasant hum of chatter from the wedding guests. She peered through the varied array of hats and hairstyles. Kirstie sat beside Alec and his wife and the bride's family. The other guests - Alissa presumed they were Simon's relatives - sat on the other side of the aisle, quietly talking among themselves.

Alissa chose to sit midway down the church. In front of her were the girls from work and the nursing staff, all turning to smile as she sat down. Mo Green signalled for Alissa to lean forward.

'Sorry I was late arriving yesterday,' she whispered. 'I had trouble with the car. What happened to the man who lost his memory?'

'We've no news yet.' Alissa shrugged. 'The police took him to Casualty for X-rays.'

'What a day!' commented Mo. 'I take it Dr Darvill won't be coming ...'

Alissa was prevented from replying by a burst of organ music and she settled back in her seat. It still hurt to think that Max had abandoned their plans. She would have accepted his decision if he had told her himself, but leaving the message with one of the reception staff she found inexcusable.

That, Alissa realised now, had been a painful reminder of the pattern of events which had defined her marriage. The memory of the bitter disappointment she had suffered over the years was still close to the surface and, no doubt, had been as much the cause of her tears yesterday as had her feelings towards Max. But the similarity in events was too distinct not to notice. In cancelling their weekend together, what clearer indication could she have had of Max's attitude towards his ex-wife?

Alissa was aware that someone had taken their place beside her. She had been deep in thought and hadn't noticed the murmur of voices around her. Distractedly she looked up and turned to glance at the late arrival.

'Hello,' Max whispered as he settled himself beside her. His silvery gaze drifted down to her face and his fingers linked over her wrist in a firm grasp.

'Max ... But you're not supposed to be here ...' She realised everyone had turned to look at them.

'Bas seems better this morning.' He bent his head, speaking quietly. 'Mrs Dunphy seems to have everything under control.'

'I didn't know he was unwell,' Alissa breathed.

Max frowned. 'Yes. I asked Ruth to pass on a message to you last night. Didn't you get it?'

'I was told that you wouldn't be able to come,' Alissa said hesitantly, remembering her swift exit from the surgery.

'Bas started an asthma attack about teatime yesterday,' Max continued. 'I knew you'd understand that something happening to one of the boys would be the only reason that would prevent me from seeing you. I told Ruth to let you know I would do my best to get here. It all depended on Bas.' He looked at her with a frown. 'I tried to ring you this morning but got no reply.'

'I left early to deliver Sasha to her friend's house, then I collected Kirstie,' Alissa explained, wondering why she hadn't realised that one of the boys might be unwell. Instead, she had fled the surgery before listening to the rest of what Ruth had to say.

Alissa inhaled his scent and her heart beat faster as she gazed at him in astonishment. He looked so handsome in his formal grey suit and white shirt, his sleeve touching her bare skin. He reached out for her hand and squeezed her fingers in his. 'So ... it was because of Bas you thought you might not be able to come today?' she murmured softly.

He looked at her in surprise. 'Of course it was. What other reason could there be?'

'I thought ...' she began, then shrugged as she met his gaze, fearing he would see the truth written in her eyes.

Suddenly the organ changed key and the music lifted into the rafters. 'Almost time,' Max whispered and, careless of who might observe the intimate gesture, he slid her hand around his arm, pressing it firmly against his sleeve as they waited for the entrance of the bride.

CHAPTER 21

EVERYONE WAITED ANXIOUSLY as the organ played on. Alissa managed to focus her mind, although the feel of Max's fingers around hers had the disturbing effect of making concentration almost impossible.

It was Max, finally, who brought her back to earth. His frown deepening, he whispered, 'I think there must be something wrong.'

Erin had not yet appeared and the organ music was beginning to sound repetitive. People began to whisper, and heads turned. Glancing at Max, Alissa sighed. 'I hope nothing has happened to Erin's car on the way here.'

Max glanced at the gold watch on his wrist. 'We're twenty minutes late.' Ten minutes later Kate Brooks, the younger of Erin's sisters, walked down the aisle in her rosebud pink bridesmaid's dress. Together with the vicar and Erin's father, they turned to face the congregation.

By the pale and anxious expression on their faces, it was clear something had happened. There was silence in the Minster as the vicar cleared his throat. 'I am deeply sorry to have to announce that, as the groom has failed to attend, the service is cancelled,' he said, looking visibly shaken. 'You must all be aware of how distressing this is for the bride and her family. However, they have suggested you continue on to the reception. I hope you will all do so.'

It was a moment or two before anyone stirred, as though no one had understood what the vicar had said. Alissa watched Mr Brooks and his daughter hurry back down the aisle, avoiding the curious glances as they went. The vicar began to talk in hushed tones to the relatives in the front pews.

'Whatever could have happened to Simon?' Alissa said to Max. 'Surely at this late stage he couldn't have changed his mind?'

'I don't think he can ever have made it up,' Max said darkly. 'After all, what excuse can there be for failing to turn up at your own wedding?'

Alissa was sitting with Erin in the hotel suite, wishing she could console her distraught friend. But, as Erin tried to recover from the terrible shock, there seemed few words Alissa could think of to say.

Erin had taken off her beloved white dress and sat in her robe, her eyes red and puffy. Kate and Mrs Brooks were doing their best. The hotel had brought tea and the manager had expressed his concern, offering to help in any way he could.

'Your father has explained to everyone,' Mrs Brooks said after a while, 'but I've had to stop him from driving to London and confronting Simon. How could he do this to you?'

It was a question everyone had been asking themselves, Alissa realised as she looked at Erin. Just a brief message telephoned to the rectory - a few words which had brought Erin's dreams crumbling around her feet as she'd stood in her bridal gown at the entrance to the church.

Alissa listened as Erin's mother spoke, but she knew that no words of comfort would help. Erin was being incredibly brave but Alissa wasn't surprised when she rose from her chair and asked to be given a few moments alone before dressing and coming downstairs to face her guests.

Alissa joined Max in the dining room where the guests were assembled, the atmosphere feeling more like a wake than a wedding.

People talked in muted tones, the topic of conversation only too obvious from the expressions on their faces.

Kirstie hurried over to join Max and Alissa. 'Is Erin all right? Can we help in any way?'

'She'll be down in a moment,' Alissa said quietly. 'I think all we can do is try to help her through this by not asking too many questions.'

Kirstie nodded. 'Of course. I'll warn the girls.' She glanced at the four banquet tables draped in white tablecloths and decorated with silver and glassware. 'Just look at all this! How could her fiancee possibly allow this to happen?'

'Is there anything I can do?' Max asked Alissa when they were alone.

Alissa shook her head. 'I don't think so. I'm sure Erin will want to get this over with as quickly as possible.' She steeled herself as she saw the lonely figure of Erin appear in the doorway.

Max had the final word. 'It will only be time that helps. I'm afraid,' he said quietly, 'and even in years to come the memory of this day will hurt like hell.'

The countryside looked achingly beautiful. Too beautiful for such a sad day, Alissa thought as she stared wordlessly out of the car window. The fields and trees were a luscious green and the sky an unblemished backdrop of blue. Max had just driven her home to collect an overnight case and Alissa was deep in thought as they sped along the country lanes towards Salisbury. She was only brought back to reality when, at a lay-by, Max turned in and switched off the engine. 'Look, even at this point,' he said quietly as she turned to stare at him, 'I'll understand if you want to turn back. What happened this morning has affected us all. I'm quite willing to call this off if you think it's best.'

Alissa hesitated, noticing the lines of deep concern etched across his face. He looked genuinely distressed for Erin.

'We chose a bad time,' Alissa acknowledged, 'but what would it resolve if we returned? There's nothing we can do for Erin.'

He nodded slowly, then reached out and covered her hand with his own. 'Just as long as you don't feel you have to do this.'

She shook her head. 'I'm looking forward to the break.'

They exchanged glances and as Max started the engine the gloomy atmosphere seemed to lift.

By three o'clock they had reached the hotel, a lovely mock-Tudor building in the heart of the countryside. In the heat of the July afternoon the cool entrance hall was a joy to stand in, and as the receptionist gave them their keys Alissa resisted the urge to smile as Max took them, looking slightly uncomfortable as he signed the register. What name had he signed? she wondered as they were shown up the creaky staircase.

'I'm getting too old for all this,' Max said as they finally stood alone in the room. 'Mr and Mrs Grey sounded all right over the phone, but I almost forgot when I signed in.'

Alissa laughed. Suddenly it felt wonderful to be with him and perfectly right. She was sad for Erin, but there was nothing more they could do at the moment. Max had reserved a lovely room. Low beams, a canopied bed and windows opening onto the countryside - what could have been more romantic?

Before she could speak, Max took her hand and led her to the window. He unlocked the catch and pushed it open. Fresh air flooded in and Alissa gasped.

'Oh, Max, this place is beautiful!'

'No,' he corrected as he turned to her. 'You are beautiful.'

She thought of her years of feeling second best, of her self-image which had been eroded during her marriage to Mike, maybe because Fiona had been a younger woman and undoubtedly beautiful - intelligent, too. Or maybe it hadn't been Fiona at all but her own deep insecurities which had made her all too aware of her failure to make her husband happy.

Now Max was telling her she was beautiful and she wanted to believe him, wanted to be beautiful for him - but was it true?

He ran his hand over her shoulders and up into her hair, sifting it through his fingers. 'I'm hungry,' he said, and, pulling her against his chest, added softly, 'but not for food. I'm ravenous for this breathtaking woman in my arms.'

CHAPTER 22

ALISSA LAY in the circle of Max's arms, staring up at the ivory canopy above her. Fingers of light stole through the fine weave, the lace frills dancing lightly in the breeze from the open window.

Their love-making had been an urgent release which neither had expected. Even the events of the day hadn't tempered their passion. Max had undressed her, letting the silk dress fall to the floor, joined swiftly by her dainty white briefs and camisole. He had slipped the silk straps from her shoulders, his fingers lingering over their delicacy, shaking slightly as he'd bent his head to kiss her freed breasts. Along the way he had shed his clothes and they lay with hers, abandoned on the floor.

Her breath had been taken away at the sight of his strong, lean body with not an ounce of excess fat. His skin was as deeply tanned as hers, pale golden. Their bodies had been burning, their embraces urgent, fingers some-times clumsy in their haste to undress and caress. All the while, he had whispered to her, reassured her, and her desire had mounted.

Slowly she'd responded until at last he'd paused and with one brief questioning glance had entered her as she'd given her silent assent. Unbelievably she'd reached that one mind-blowing moment shortly before he'd lost control. Together they'd arched and cried aloud, her release so sudden and unexpected that she'd been unaware of his.

Only in the gentle kisses he'd placed on her neck as his taut body had relaxed beside her had she understood his complete fulfilment. Together they lay, surprised and exhausted that their passion had been so equally shared.

Now, his elbow dug into the pillow, his head propped on his hand, he stared at her, studying her face. She watched his lips twitch, beguiled and fascinated by the way they turned up at the corners in a quizzical smile.

'What are you thinking?' he whispered, narrowing his eyes as though trying to read her mind.

'Selfishly,' she told him, 'I was thinking just how wonderful I feel.'

He looked at her with concern. 'No regrets ...?'

She smiled. 'None. Have you?'

'Only one,' he said quietly as he gazed at her. 'That I haven't had the courage to ask you to come away with me before.'

'Did you want to?' she asked, half smiling.

'Oh, yes.' He chuckled, his grey eyes dancing over her face. 'Shall I tell you a secret?'

'Only if it's a nice one.' She laughed softly as he pulled her to him and kissed her playfully.

'Do you remember that first time, when we went to Shermore Manor? I knew then that I wanted to make love to you. It was as though I were seeing everything through new eyes - the colours, the people, the noises, the smells.

It was all I could do to take my eyes off you, to concentrate on what we were doing and where we were going. Although I had been there before, the place was new to me.' A smile touched his lips. 'I didn't want that day to end.'

She reached up to draw her fingers over his cheek. 'That's a lovely thing to say, Max.'

'It's true. Just like I never want this day to end.' He took her in his arms and kissed her until she responded with the same, uninhibited hunger.

Their love-making changed this time, their awareness of the release of their emotions freeing them from convention and, despite the darkening shadows settling across the late afternoon sky, they became lost in their own world, their bodies and minds filled with one longing. Each other.

CHAPTER 23

It was dusk when they woke from a sound, almost unreal sleep. Max held her in his arms and they lay quietly, listening to the sounds of the hotel and the late chorus of birds in the trees below. They decided they needed to eat and showered and dressed in casual clothes.

Alissa wore an ankle-length shift in a creamy colour with a halter neckline. Max chose lightweight trousers and a crisp blue cotton shirt. Phone calls home revealed all was well. Sasha and Amy were fast asleep. The party had been a roaring success, reported Caroline Lewis. If Alissa was agreeable, she and her husband would like to take the girls to the beach for the day tomorrow. Alissa accepted, selfishly welcoming the extra time it would provide with Max.

Mrs Dunphy had encountered no problems with Bas and he, too, was asleep. With their calls made, they ate a light meal of salad and sole followed by cheese and biscuits in one of the hotel bars, the restaurant having long since closed.

Locals arrived and the hotel guests meandered in and out of the bar. When the time came to leave, they delayed the moment when they would fall into each other's arms and left the hotel to stroll along the riverbank.

In the silk-soft evening, Max kissed her and she threaded her arms around his neck, gazing into the deep pools of silver half hidden in shadow. She realised that neither of them wanted to talk, not now, for the quickening of her body made her want him again and she knew her need was reciprocated. As tiny grey clouds masked the moon's light, they retraced their steps to the hotel.

Ascending the creaky staircase, they trod softly along the carpeted landing. Max paused as he slid the key in the lock and bent to kiss her as they stood on the threshold of their room. Seconds later he lifted her into his arms and carried her across the floor to their canopied bed.

Hours later, Alissa awoke, knowing she had cried out in her sleep. She'd been dreaming of Mike. He had been there in front of her, quite clearly, as though he'd been standing in the room. Then suddenly the dream had changed to the scene of the accident, the car eaten up like some fragile toy under the wheels of the pantechnicon.

Her body was bathed in perspiration. Her mind tried to detach itself from the unreal to the present and the early morning light streaming in through unfamiliar brocade curtains. Slowly she remembered where she was and, turning her head on the pillow, lifted her eyes to see that Max was awake beside her.

'It's all right,' he told her, drawing her towards him. 'You were dreaming.'

She swallowed, moistening her dry lips. 'Did I wake you?'

'I was awake,' he told her, and she nodded slowly, her eyes taking in the reassuring sight of the man beside her. For the very first time she noticed the small lines running from eyes to hairline, travelling up into the finest of silver hairs, normally too fine to be seen when brushed back and hidden in the thick pelt of dark hair.

He drew the tip of his finger over her lips, smoothing it softly through the veil of perspiration lying on her brow. 'I don't think I'll ever get used to looking at you,' he whispered, 'or to thinking how lovely you are, or to seeing something about you that I hadn't noticed before.'

She didn't know how to react, only that she felt overwhelmed as a wave of emotion flowed through her. He saw confusion in her expression and whispered, 'Was it a very bad dream?'

She curled against him, taking comfort from his embrace. 'It was one I have every so often ... of Mike and the accident. It seems so real. I'm there, watching it happen.' He was silent for a moment then spoke as though with relief. 'Thank God you and Sasha weren't in the car, too.'

'There was never any danger of that,' she said huskily. 'Mike wouldn't have taken us. He had gone back to Kent to ... to see Fiona.'

'His secretary?'

'And mistress.' Alissa's voice was a whisper. 'They'd been involved before we were married. Fiona was the reason we moved to Hayford Minster.'

Max held her away from him. 'But why didn't you tell me this before?'

'I ... I'm not sure. I've never told anyone. And, to be honest, I've tried not to think about it for Sasha's sake. I only want her to know the best about her father.'

'But you must have been hurt - deeply,' he muttered, frowning. 'Weren't you?'

She nodded. 'Of course. But I believed him when he promised to stop seeing her. And then, when I realised it would be impossible for him to give her up while we still lived in Kent, I knew we had to move. I thought it was our only chance.'

He drew her to him and hugged her tightly. 'My God, what could have possessed the man to fall for someone else when he had you?'

Alissa shook her head slowly. 'He seemed to be able to love us both, in different ways. He couldn't decide what he wanted - who he wanted.'

'And the affair still went on after Sasha was born?'

She bit her lip, closing her eyes, the emotion threatening to break through. He waited silently, giving her time to go on, as for the first time in years she admitted the truth of her doomed marriage. 'Fiona phoned him one weekend,' she went on shakily. 'Mike told me he was going to see her, though I begged him not to - until I realised that the move from Kent hadn't worked either. Instead, her absence was separating us. I knew I had to let him go.'

'And the accident happened on the way back?'

'Yes.' She choked back her tears. 'If we hadn't moved from London, he'd still be alive today. Sasha would still have her father.'

'But you weren't responsible for the accident. Neither were you responsible for the way he felt about Fiona. You can't blame yourself for things that were out of your control.' He pulled her closer and looked into her eyes. 'Listen to me, you did nothing wrong. You have nothing to feel guilty about.'

This time she sought physical comfort from him with a desperate need of her own. It drew from him an equal response, as if the catharsis had fused them in a way that had not been open to them before.

Without words, they claimed the reassurance they needed, bodies united together with a passion that only true lovers generated. Finally they lay exhausted, entangled amongst the damp sheets, and fell asleep.

CHAPTER 24

LATER THAT MORNING Max ordered coffee to be brought up to their room. They lingered over the drink, lazing on the bed, with the windows thrown open to the fresh country air. Alissa wondered if they really had passed the night in each other's arms, but when she saw Max walk from the shower half an hour later, his wet hair thrust back over his head, his strong body glistening with tiny pearls of water, she recalled the exquisite moments of their love-making.

After breakfast at the hotel they drove to Salisbury, drank lemonade mixed with fresh orange juice under the umbrellas of a market square cafe and found another quiet riverbank to rest on.

They reclined on the warm grass, talking about anything and everything, watched the swans and the lazy procession of afternoon tourists, kissed briefly when they thought they were alone.

When Max took her hand and pulled her against him, she knew they had to be leaving soon. 'I could stay here like this for another week,' he murmured, and she nodded.

'It's been lovely, Max.'

'Shall we do it again some time?' He moved and she looked up at him, wondering if there really would be another time.

'I'd like to, yes,' she replied quietly. Their eyes met and in his she saw a reflection of herself, a woman in love. Her heart beat fast and he leaned forward to kiss her as a hunger, intense and deep, welled up inside her.

CHAPTER 25

ERIN TORE the circulars in half and threw them in the bin liner. Twirling the little wire tag around the neck of the plastic bag, she left it beside the wheely-bin ready for disposal.

In almost a fortnight, she had filled several such bags. All the rubbish had gone. The small pieces of furniture she had bought for the cottage were to be sent for auction next week. She had returned the wedding gifts with a brief note of apology. Now she would close this painful chapter on her life and try to start afresh.

She gazed from the cottage window at the overgrown garden she'd intended to turn into a flower-filled paradise. Had it all really been her dream and not Simon's? The few weekends she and Simon had spent decorating the cottage could hardly count as memories. Simon had never really had his heart in it, even as recently as the week before the wedding when he'd avoided their last rehearsal, claiming he had a cold. Cold feet, more aptly, she thought bitterly.

Now the cottage was going back on the market and she hoped that the place would bring someone else the happiness that had eluded her. A knock on the front door made her jump and, closing the leaded window in the kitchen, she went to answer it. The stable door creaked open as she slid the bolt. She peered out to see Alissa standing there, her eyebrows raised.

'I saw your car, Erin. Is there anything I can do to help? Or am I calling at a bad moment?'

'Oh, no - come in, please.' Erin was relieved it was Alissa and not one of the neighbours who, well intentioned as they might be, were curious at the 'for sale' notice in the garden. 'I'm just locking up and going back to the flat.'

'Has anyone been to view the cottage yet?' Alissa entered and followed Erin into the front room.

'It's early days.' Erin sat on a wooden wheel-back chair and gestured for Alissa to sit on the other. 'The estate agents said it will sell quite quickly once they've processed the brochures.'

'It is a lovely place.' Alissa gazed around the room.

Erin nodded. 'I thought so. Obviously Simon didn't.' Alissa frowned. 'How are you feeling now?'

Erin shrugged. 'Still confused. He can't explain why he did it. There's no one else apparently. He says he still loves me, but that he couldn't make the break from London. Obviously he didn't love me enough to leave his life there.'

Alissa sighed and for a moment or two they sat in silence. 'What will you do now?' she asked eventually.

'Oh, return to work on Monday,' Erin answered with another casual shrug. 'Two weeks off has been enough time to deal with the sale of the cottage and to be with my family. All I want to do now is get on with my life.' Alissa smiled. 'We've missed you.'

'And I've missed the practice.' Erin squared her shoulders. 'So, what's been happening while I've been away?'

As Alissa told her about Alec's slow recovery from his fall downstairs and some of the other things that had been happening at the surgery, Erin longed for the comforting routine of work to help ease the ache and loneliness inside her. These past two weeks, which should have been the happiest time of her life - her honeymoon - had been the bleakest ever.

They talked a while longer until finally Alissa had to leave for her calls. Erin walked with her to the car and was about to say goodbye when her gaze landed on a pair of football boots on the rear seat. 'Is Sasha in the football team now?' she remarked, half joking.

'Oh, no.' Alissa hesitated. 'They belong to Bas. We...er...gave him a lift home from a football match a couple of nights ago.'

Erin nodded slowly, unable to resist smiling. 'How is Max?' she asked.

'Oh - fine.' Not meeting her gaze, Alissa unlocked the car and was on the point of climbing in when she seemed to change her mind and allowed the door to close. She sank back against it with a deep sigh. 'You've guessed, haven't you?'

Erin nodded. 'About you and Max? Yes.'

'Is it that obvious?'

'Only to someone who knows you both well.' Erin paused. 'Is it supposed to be a secret?'

Alissa frowned. 'Neither of us wants to commit to anything serious - we both have busy lives. At the moment we've decided to take one day at a time.' She sighed softly. 'Though time is often the factor that's missing.'

Erin smiled thoughtfully. 'You know, privately, I've always suspected Max needed someone to anchor him. He's a married man at heart, definitely not a natural single parent, despite his capability with the boys.'

'To be honest,' Alissa said quietly, 'I've always thought Max is still - married - in an odd kind of way.'

'Oh, you mean ...' Erin hesitated, raising her eyebrows. 'Priss?'

Alissa nodded. 'Yes.'

Erin thought how, if the positions were reversed, she might well feel the same as Alissa. Priss was a determined woman. On the surface it looked as though she wanted Max back again, but was he still in love with her - enough to take her back?

Erin decided there was no clear answer. Her own recent misfortune with Simon hardly qualified her to offer advice, even if she'd known what was going on in Max's mind, which she didn't.

'Well, I'll be on my way,' Alissa said at last. Leaning forward, she kissed Erin on the cheek. 'See you Monday, then. And let me know if there's anything I can do to help in the meantime.'

Erin nodded and watched Alissa drive off. Turning back to the cottage, she walked down the garden path, slowly turning the conversation over in her mind. She had drawn comfort from her friend's visit.

Things could have been worse. At least Simon hadn't married her and then made the decision to leave her!

CHAPTER 26

ON THE THURSDAY after Erin returned to work Alissa received a phone call from the police. Mrs Bowen, the elderly lady she and Max had helped in the taxi, had died in hospital of a coronary thrombosis. It was a shock Alissa wasn't prepared for, although the police assured her that Mrs Bowen's death didn't appear to be linked to the injuries she'd sustained in the accident.

The following day, Friday, Alissa was in her room, studying a letter she'd received in the post, when Jane knocked on her door and entered. 'The police phoned just as I arrived here earlier this morning,' Jane told her. 'They asked me to explain that Eamon Jeffs, the taxi driver who lost his memory, won't be charged with any offence concerning the accident. It seems that before she died Mrs Bowen made a full statement. Apparently the cause of the accident was a deer which had strayed into the road. Mrs Bowen said that Mr Jeffs swerved, trying to avoid it.'

'I see.' Alissa passed the letter she was holding to Jane. 'I hope that news will help Mr and Mrs Jeffs. He still can't remember everything, according to this. His wife is worried about him. He's unable to drive, she writes.' Jane sighed as she read the letter. 'She's asking you to see him, hoping that returning to the surgery might jog his memory.'

'I'm not sure that would be wise. He's under Mr Holings, a neurologist, who has referred him for a psychiatric report.'

Jane frowned. 'Oh, dear. Does that mean he has some mental problem?'

'It's something they have to check out,' Alissa explained. 'The block obviously hasn't been helped by Mrs Bowen's death.'

'You mean he may feel responsible?'

Alissa nodded. 'It's possible.'

The secretary handed back Mrs Jeffs's letter. 'Well, I'd better get on.' She paused. 'Oh, by the way, I saw Jamie Atkins the other day.'

Alissa looked up. 'Did you? Where?'

'In Oxford Street, of all places.' Jane shrugged. 'I'd gone up to London for the weekend to visit my sister and was doing some shopping. And there was Jamie, hailing a cab. He didn't see me, but it was definitely him.'

'Was he on his own?'

Jane nodded. 'Odd, isn't it?'

Alissa had to agree. From the way Betty had spoken Alissa had formed the impression that Jamie was always hard at work on the farm with no time to spare. After Jane had gone, Alissa finished her early morning coffee and, making a mental note to discuss Jamie with Max once more, she began her surgery.

Her first patient provided yet another surprise. 'Hello, Dr Leigh,' said India, guiding a pushchair into the room.

'India - I've been wondering about you.' Alissa gestured to the seat by her desk. 'Are you both well? How is Orion?'

'Much better,' the girl said quietly. 'I'm taking him to Outpatients for another check in a week's time.' She had gained a little weight, Alissa thought, and Orion, asleep in his pushchair, looked rosy-cheeked. 'I thought I'd let you know that the caravans are being moved on today,' India went on, not quite meeting Alissa's gaze. 'I've decided to stay in Hayford Minster. I've got a place to stay in town - only one room, but it will do for now.'

'And Sky?' Alissa asked, guessing the answer.

'We've split up. It happened that day I last saw you. When he finally came back to the caravan we had another awful row over Orion. He said if that was the way I felt, letting doctors have their way, then I didn't trust him to look after us, especially as I want Orion to have all his vaccinations. Mum was right. I see it now. But I didn't realise how I'd feel ...' She looked down at her sleeping child. 'I moved out from the caravan and Sky's going on with the travellers.'

'I'm sorry to hear that.' Alissa felt sad for India as she sat there, pushing back her narrow shoulders in an effort to look determined. 'Is there no hope you'll be able to get together later on?'

'I don't think so.' India's lips trembled. 'I've got Orion to think of now. And that kind of life isn't for us. Orion's health is important. I'd feel terrible if something happened to him.'

Alissa felt both regret and relief for the tiny child curled in the pushchair. It was, she thought, a sign of the times that the future was increasingly uncertain for young people like these.

'My name is really Esme Kelly,' India told her. 'I've given all my details to your receptionist and I've booked Orion to have his jabs next week.'

Alissa nodded. 'Have you any friends in Hayford Minster?'

'No. But we'll manage.' The girl rose and guided the pushchair to the door. 'Bye, then. Dr Leigh.'

Was there any hope of convincing Sky to remain with his family? Alissa wondered as India turned into the corridor. In the unlikely event the travellers were still at Hayford Minster Wood after her surgery, she would take a chance and call on Sky in a last effort to persuade him to change his mind.

The rest of the day was unbelievably busy. Her surgery comprised holiday-makers and residents, a number of children still attending the allergy clinic and several pregnant women, requiring their monthly checks.

By five she had finally completed her list. The familiar knock on the door she had half expected all day came as she was preparing to leave. Max entered and, closing the door softly behind him, grinned as he came towards her. Without speaking, he bent to kiss her. 'That's better,' he sighed, and sank into the chair beside her desk. 'Now I can concentrate.'

She laughed, her cheeks flushed. 'Busy day?' 'Midsummer madness,' he commented dryly. 'Compounded by the school holidays and all those complaints no one seems to want to resolve during term time.'

'Talking of term time,' Alissa asked, 'how is Mrs Dunphy coping during the holiday?'

He arched an eyebrow. 'Aaron makes himself scarce, no doubt spending most of his time with Clare. His fifteenth birthday comes up at the end of August. He's asked if he can have a disco in the garden.'

'Really?' Alissa smiled. 'That sounds like fun.'

'Do you think so?' Max's expression was wry. 'In that case, would you like to spend the day with us and lend a hand?'

Alissa was taken by surprise. 'Are you sure?'

'Absolutely.'

After their weekend away, their moments of intimacy were rare since their meetings always always came secondary to the welfare of the children. Bearing in mind that Sasha and Bas often suggested shared outings and were eager to spend time together, the children had accepted their relationship.

However, Aaron's birthday was a family event and she wondered what his response to her presence at the party would be. Almost as if reading her mind. Max smiled and without a word reached across to smooth his thumb across her lips. 'I miss you,' he whispered huskily. 'I see you every day, but I still miss you.'

Later, Alissa drove home past Hayford Minster Wood. The travellers had abandoned their site, only the bleached grass and a few pieces of litter remaining where their vehicles had been parked.

Dismayed that she hadn't been able to attempt one last effort to reunite the family, Alissa drove around the bend on which Eamon Jeffs's taxi had left the road. Much had happened in that short space of time. India, or rather Esme Kelly, had made a decision that had changed the future for herself and young Orion. Eamon Jeffs had suffered the loss of his memory and was struggling to come to terms with what had happened as a result. Mrs Bowen had never taken that flight from Heathrow to see her daughter. And Betty and Jamie Atkins's lives were even more deeply embedded in mystery than they had been six months ago.

And Erin - poor Erin! Her friend and colleague's plight raised questions which Alissa still found disturbing. As she drove on towards Green Gables she realised there were personal questions she had been considering for a long time now. What of the future for herself and Max? He was becoming more a part of her life by the day, despite her efforts to keep him at a distance. She couldn't forget the past and her experience with Mike and Fiona should serve to remind her that Max might never be prepared to distance himself from Priss.

As Alissa turned into the drive, she saw Sasha and Astrid sitting on the front lawn, a blanket spread beneath them on the grass. They waved as she drove up. She gave a toot on the horn in response. Everything she loved and valued was here - her home, her daughter, the security she had worked so hard to achieve since Mike's death. Despite the assurance Max had given her that he tolerated Priss's unpredictable behaviour only for the sake of the boys, her fears that this wasn't so were deepening.

On the following Wednesday Alissa was about to leave the surgery at lunchtime when Keeley Summers signalled her to the desk. Keeley covered the telephone with her hand and mouthed, 'It's for you, Dr Leigh. I think it's a child.'

Alissa took the receiver. 'Hello, Dr Leigh speaking.' For a few seconds there was silence then she heard a half whisper, half sob. Alissa repeated herself, but the line went dead.

Alissa leaned across to Keeley, asking the receptionist to dial the number required to trace the previous caller. Keeley did so and, taking her pen, wrote the number down.

'Hayford Minster 24683 ...' Alissa pondered, frowning at the pad.

'I know that one off by heart - the Atkinses,' said Max, appearing in the doorway with a frown of concern on his forehead.

'Yes, of course.' Alissa nodded slowly. 'I recall it now.'

'What happened?' Max asked.

Alissa shrugged. 'I'm not sure who it was, but it sounded like one of the children - on the other hand, it might have been a practical joke.'

'I don't think so,' remarked Keeley, 'because whoever it was tried to get through before but I could barely get a word out of them.'

'I think I'd better drive out there,' Alissa decided.

'I'll drive you.' Max glanced at Keeley. 'Keep ringing the number, will you, Keeley? If you manage to speak to anyone and they're in difficulty, tell them we're on our way.'

'Do you want me to ring the police, too?' Keeley asked.

Alissa shook her head. 'Not yet. It may be a false alarm. We'll let you know when we reach the farm.'

Alissa found herself holding onto her seat as Max drove swiftly through the country lanes. When they finally arrived at the farm and parked, the place looked deserted. Machinery lay idle in the shed, the barn doors were open, revealing an empty hay loft. The place was deserted. Nearing the farmhouse, Alissa saw that one of the windows was broken.

The door opened as they approached and there in the hallway was Emily. Her cheeks were tear-stained and Alissa knelt and took her into her arms, giving the little girl a hug. 'It's all right, Emily. We're here now,' she soothed. 'Can you take us to Mummy?'

Emily nodded and led them into the back garden. Going by way of a side gate to the dairy, they found the yard empty. At the far end of the dairy Emily pointed to a shed where the corrugated roof had collapsed. 'Mummy,' said Emily, her chin wobbling.

'In there?' asked Max, and the little girl nodded.

'Watch out for splinters of metal,' Max warned as he stepped forward and lifted several of the pieces to one side. It didn't take them long to clear the debris, and as the last piece came away a shower of dust exploded around them.

Betty lay on the floor at the back of the shed, her face white. 'The r-roof collapsed on me,' she sobbed as they hurried to kneel beside her.

'Are you hurt?' Max asked as he helped her to lean back against some sacking and began to examine her.

She shook her head. 'I don't think so. I managed to crawl into the corner. I was trying to find some boarding for the broken window at the front of the house. I didn't realise the roof was in such a bad state.'

'But where's Jamie?' Alissa frowned. 'Shouldn't you have waited for him?'

At this, Betty's face crumpled and tears trickled down her cheeks. 'Jamie's left me.'

'He's *what?*' said Max as they looked at Betty in astonishment.

Betty swallowed then looked up at them. 'Jamie walked out four months ago. I've been trying to manage on my own, without telling anyone. I thought he might change his mind ...'

Alissa took a tissue from her pocket and handed it to Betty. She blew her nose and wiped her eyes. 'He comes back to see the children, but we quarrel all the time. He says he's fed up with farming and there's no future in it. He sold the herd and rented the fields out. He's looking for a nine-to-five job with a pay packet at the end of it.' She sighed as she took a deep breath. 'That's why I wanted help with Emily. I just couldn't cope alone. Emily misses him the most and was driving me to distraction, asking for her daddy all the time. I just didn't know what to do for the best.'

Max said nothing, his brow furrowed as he listened to the baby's heartbeat. Finally he removed the stethoscope and, glancing at Betty, raised his eyebrows. 'The baby's heartbeat isn't quite one hundred and twenty - I'd like to see it up a bit. We need to get you in hospital and make sure everything's all right. Where are the other children?'

'Donna and Mark are with Jamie,' Betty answered shakily. 'When he visits he takes two of the children at a time. Sam's in his cot.'

Leaving Max to attend to Betty, Alissa grasped Emily's hand and went back to the house. She rang for an ambulance then went up to Sam who was curled in his cot. He woke at her entrance and she lifted him into her arms.

'I'm hungry,' Emily said. Relieved that Emily had an appetite, she took the children downstairs and settled them at the big pine table.

When Sam was safely in his high chair she asked them what they would like to eat.

'Fish fingers!' Emily pointed to the freezer and, clapping his hands, Sam squealed as Alissa took them from the compartment.

By the time the ambulance arrived, Emily and Sam were eating their meal contentedly, unaware of the activity in the yard. Just as Alissa was wondering when Jamie would return she heard the front door open and Jamie and the children walked in. 'What's happening here?' he demanded as he saw Alissa.

Before she could respond his face went white as his gaze travelled beyond her through the window to the yard. 'Oh, my God,' he groaned as he saw his wife's supine body lying on a stretcher, two burly paramedics lifting it into the ambulance.

At half past eight that evening, Max and Alissa left the maternity wing of Hayford Cottage Hospital. Max stretched his arms and rubbed his hands over his face as they walked towards the Discovery. 'Do you think this episode will bring Betty and Jamie to their senses?' he asked her.

'I hope so,' Alissa answered doubtfully. 'There's no doubt that Betty will stay in here until the delivery and Jamie is going to have to pull his weight with the children.'

'He looked exhausted,' Max said as he opened the door for her and she climbed in. 'He's been looking for jobs all over the place, apparently.'

Alissa nodded. 'Yes, Jane said she'd seen him in London.'

'Not easy for a veteran farmer who knows very little else,' observed Max as he closed her door. When he climbed in beside her he frowned, pausing before he started the engine. 'What I still can't make out is why Betty went to such lengths to convince us nothing had happened between them.'

Alissa looked at him and sighed softly. 'I suppose we all do a little wishful thinking from time to time. It's just that Betty's got out of hand over the years.'

'Wishful thinking, yes,' agreed Max, 'but not complete fantasy.'

'She was trying to keep her family together,' Alissa said. 'It's understandable if you think about it.'

'By deceiving Jamie?'

'Oh, there's no excuse for that, I agree. Her motives were selfish, yes, but she loved him. That would be a forgivable offence in some people's eyes.'

Max held her gaze. 'Does love really conquer all, then?' Alissa looked away, suddenly chilled as the evening breeze blew in through the open window. Love hadn't conquered all in the case of her marriage to Mike. He'd needed her but had loved Fiona. Her throat tightened as for a moment the memory of Mike and Fiona in each other's arms passed before her eyes.

'Alissa?' Max was staring at her. 'Are you all right?' She blinked, looking back at him. 'Oh - yes. Sorry, what were you saying?'

He reached out and touched her cheek, drawing his fingers softly over her skin, his grey eyes questioning hers. 'Nothing important. I'll drive you home,' he murmured with a quiet finality that made her suspect that tonight they wouldn't delay their goodbyes as they usually did, lengthening each moment before they kissed and said goodnight. Tonight they would go their separate ways, each with their own thoughts.

CHAPTER 27

AT THE NEXT PRACTICE MEETING, midway through August, Alec confirmed his intention to retire at Christmas. Kirstie James called an extraordinary meeting the following week. The difficulties in finding a suitable replacement were obvious, Alissa realised as she listened to Kirstie's comments. Alec's list included patients he had treated for over thirty years and his presence would be deeply missed.

On the following Wednesday morning halfway through surgery Erin knocked and entered her room, clearly distressed. 'It's Hannah Brent,' she explained. 'She has severe rhinitis and a rash, but I'm afraid I feel rather unwell at the moment ...'

'Would you like me to see Hannah?' Alissa asked at once.

'If you've time.' Erin hesitated. 'Are you busy?'

'I've no one waiting at the moment,' Alissa reassured her.

Erin sighed. 'I'm afraid you'll find Mrs Brent rather a difficult lady.'

On her way along the corridor Alissa met Max and told him what had happened. Since he was also waiting for his next patient, he offered to remain with Erin. A few moments later Alissa found herself trying to determine what had caused Hannah Brent's hay fever and the unpleasant rash on the eight-year-old's arms and neck.

'We never have convenience food,' Mrs Brent protested as Alissa asked what Hannah had eaten that day. 'And she hasn't been playing in the garden. Last time we came Dr Brooks seemed to think the rash was to do with nettles.'

'But that's ridiculous! It's happened again and Hannah has been with me all morning in the house.'

Alissa studied the angry red blotches that marked Hannah's pale skin. 'If Hannah isn't allergic to something in her diet,' she explained, 'then it must be an external problem - for instance, washing powder or dust mites, or an allergy to animals.'

'We haven't got any pets,' Mrs Brent objected impatiently. 'And I keep the house spotless. Are you suggesting the rash is my fault?'

'No - ' Alissa began, but made little headway as Hannah's mother stiffened her shoulders and stood up. 'Come along, Hannah! We're leaving.'

'Mrs Brent,' Alissa said calmly, 'it's important we try to discover the cause of Hannah's problems. In order to do this we have to look at all the possibilities.'

'I shall be writing to the Health Service to make a complaint that I've just been passed from one doctor to another,' Mrs Brent said, ignoring Alissa's comment as she opened the door. Tugging little Hannah beside her, the tall figure of Mrs Brent strode out of the room and down the corridor.

Alissa sighed. It appeared that whatever course of action was taken with Hannah Mrs Brent refused to co-operate. When Alissa returned to her room Max was sitting with Erin and both of them looked up.

'Trouble?' asked Max as Alissa sighed and sat at her desk.

She nodded. 'I'm afraid Mrs Brent seems to take any investigation into Hannah's problem personally. Obviously Hannah has an allergy. The point is, to what? When I tried to discuss the options with her she left abruptly.'

'There's no pleasing some,' Max commented darkly. But Erin looked anxious. 'It's Hannah I'm concerned for.'

Laying a hand on Erin's drooping shoulder, Max smiled. 'Don't worry about that now. Why don't you take the afternoon off?'

Erin shook her head. 'No, Max, thanks all the same. In fact, I feel better now.' She rose, still looking pale. 'Thank you for seeing Mrs Brent for me, Alissa.'

'I'm afraid I didn't achieve very much. Are you sure you'll be all right?'

Erin nodded. 'Yes, I'll be fine now.'

When she had gone, Max closed the door quietly after her, his brow furrowed. 'I'm worried about Erin. She doesn't look her old self. Do you think this is linked to Simon?'

Alissa had no doubt that was the problem and she nodded. 'However, patients like Mrs Brent don't help very much,' she added on a sigh. 'I didn't mention this to Erin, but Mrs Brent threatened to write a letter of complaint to the authorities.'

'What exactly is her problem?' Max asked sharply. Alissa frowned. 'Amongst other things, that we have failed to discover what's wrong with Hannah.'

'From what Erin has told me,' Max replied swiftly, 'we've not been given the opportunity to find out.' He shook his head. 'After lunch I'll tell Lyn to telephone her and try to make an appointment. This time I'll see her.' Alissa had little hope that Mrs Brent would co-operate, but she nodded and for a moment they remained in silence. Then Max walked towards her and, reaching out, drew her into his arms. 'When am I going to see you next?' he whispered against her ear.

Last night, paying a late call to her house after the children were in bed, he'd stayed far later than either of them had intended. The smile that crossed his face revealed that he, too, was thinking the same as he looked into her eyes

'Were the boys asleep when you got home?' she asked with a rueful grin.

'Sleeping like tops.' He tipped her chin up and his grey eyes searched her face. 'You haven't changed your mind about Aaron's birthday?'

She shook her head. 'No ...' She added hesitantly, 'Will Priss be coming?'

'What made you ask that?'

'Well, it is Aaron's birthday -

'As a matter of fact, it isn't,' he interrupted her. 'His birthday is really on the Tuesday after, but Aaron wanted the party on the Saturday night.'

There was no time to ask more as, with perfect timing, the phone rang on her desk. Max groaned softly under his breath and let her go, lifting his eyes to hers as he opened the door of her room and departed.

Alissa paused momentarily before she answered the call, trying to collect her thoughts. It had only been last night as she'd said goodbye to him in the early hours of the morning that she'd realised she hadn't wanted to ask the question she'd just asked. She had to admit that now she knew there would be no chance of an encounter with Priss she felt better about the whole thing.

CHAPTER 28

ON THE WEDNESDAY before Aaron's party Betty Atkins gave birth to a baby boy. According to Jamie, who left a message with Reception, Betty and the baby were well, despite baby James's premature birth. There was no indication as to whether the couple had patched up their differences, but it seemed apparent that while Jamie remained at home with the children in Betty's absence the question of Emily's future had been set aside.

The next surprise came in the form of Eamon Jeffs who, the same morning, walked into Alissa's consulting room accompanied by his wife, Jean.

'He's still having trouble,' the small, neatly dressed woman told Alissa as she sat beside her husband. 'Mr Holings, Eamon's consultant, says it's due to short-term memory loss. The problem is, Eamon can't drive. He seems to have lost his nerve. That means we've no money coming in.'

Eamon Jeffs, sitting beside his wife, looked tired and dispirited. He still had no recall of the accident in early July when he'd been driving toward Hayford Minster Wood with Mrs Bowen as his passenger.

'I think,' Jean Jeffs said with a sigh, 'he blames himself for what happened to Mrs Bowen and he's blanking out the accident.'

'But Mrs Bowen died of natural causes,' Alissa said as she looked at Eamon Jeffs. 'And you swerved in order to avoid a deer, a perfectly natural reaction in the circumstances,' she added as the two people looked at her in dismay.

But Eamon Jeffs shook his head. 'That's as may be, but every time I get in my taxi I come out in a sweat. I feel terrified. I can't even switch on the engine my hands are shaking so much.'

Their discussion came to an unsatisfactory end despite Alissa's attempts to reassure him. Dejectedly the couple left. Alissa wondered if a reconstruction of the event might be helpful but thought better of it since he was still a patient under the hospital's care. She realised that for once there was absolutely nothing she could do to help. As with many psychological wounds, time would probably be the only healer.

THE WEEKEND of Aaron's party arrived and, still with some trepidation, Alissa prepared to leave. She decided to wear jeans and a casual shirt, hoping that everyone else would also be dressed informally. Sasha was wildly excited at the prospect of spending a whole day at the Darvills' and Alissa had to admit to herself that she was excited, too, despite her initial misgivings.

As they drove across town to Max's house, Alissa found herself wondering if Aaron would approve of her presence at the house on his birthday when his own mother would be absent. But she had no need to worry as by the time she arrived the preparations were in full swing. A marquee had been erected in the garden and Aaron and several of his friends were carrying out a battered old hi-fi system from the house.

'That's great, Dr Leigh. Thanks,' Aaron said when she gave him his gift, a CD which Max had told her he wanted. 'I'll play it as soon as we get the music going in the tent.' And with that he sped off, leaving Alissa to wonder what she'd been worried about.

Sasha was enthralled by the scene. 'Can I go into the tent, too, Mummy?'

Alissa nodded. 'I should think so. Don't get in the way if the boys are busy, though.'

Sasha ran off and to Alissa's amusement was met by Bas who beckoned her excitedly into the marquee. Just as Alissa was wondering what she should do with herself Max strode from the house, looking cool and casual in jeans and a denim shirt.

'Hello, there,' he called as he walked across the lawn to greet her. His mouth curved up at the corners and his eyes were warm and inviting. He didn't put his arm around her, but the smile he gave her stirred her heart. 'Mrs Dunphy asked me to bring you in for a cup of tea.' He grinned. 'I think she'll be very glad of the moral support.' He bent towards her and whispered, 'As I will.'

Alissa smiled and he looked at her for a long while, the noise seeming to fade around them as they stood there. Then, turning, they began to walk to the side entrance of the house, and before she knew it Alissa was helping in the kitchen and talking to Mrs Dunphy who had insisted on catering the party.

It was a satisfying morning, Alissa decided as she worked alongside the older woman. They talked and laughed while they worked and occasionally Max looked in to see how they were doing. By one o'clock all was finished. Mrs Dunphy thanked Alissa for her help, before hanging her apron on the back of the kitchen door and drinking her final cup of tea.

When his housekeeper had departed, Max entered the kitchen and took Alissa's hand. 'Come with me for a moment,' he said softly, arching an eyebrow. 'I want to say hello to you in private.' Her heart was racing as once inside his study he closed the door of the comfortable, book - lined room. He crossed to adjust the lateral blind, then came back to take her hand and press her against the shelves. He bent to kiss her, his mouth moving hungrily over hers. 'Oh, Lord,' he sighed, 'you taste wonderful - and I've got to behave myself for hours yet.'

He kissed her again, his lips drawing her reluctant response as her body leaned into the curve of his, her fingers running over his broad shoulders. A few months ago, she thought to herself as she surrendered to the passion that seemed to be growing day by day between them, I wouldn't have believed this possible ...

The strains of a bass guitar echoed from the garden and Max lifted his head and sighed. 'Kids!' He grinned and they laughed softly together for a moment, like conspirators. Then his hands came up to cup her face. He kissed her again, the air around them charged with electricity. His tongue flicked out to probe the corners of her mouth and she closed her eyes, surrendering to the temptation of his kiss.

'Mmm,' he whispered, 'as sweet as honey.'

The noise of the music grew louder. 'Don't you think we had better put in an appearance?' she murmured, smiling ruefully.

He nodded and, linking his fingers securely around hers, he crept out with her from their hiding place. With her heart racing, she held his hand as he led her into the garden.

'Aaron says that when they've got the music right we can dance on the grass.' Sasha sat on Alissa's lap, watching the older boys testing the hi-fi system. Surrounding them were a dozen picnic chairs and plastic tables positioned in a semicircle around the area designated for dancing.

The buffet was set on two trestle tables at the far end and some more boys and girls who had arrived were hanging balloons from the poles of the marquee.

Alissa hugged her daughter. 'Are you having a good time, darling?'
Sasha nodded enthusiastically. 'Mummy, do you like Dr Darvill?'
Alissa nodded. 'Yes, of course I do.'
'I think he's nice, too. Mummy?'
Alissa smiled, guessing what was coming next. 'Yes?'
'Do you think Dr Darvill likes us?'
Alissa nodded again. 'I hope so.'
'Only Bas says - 'But Sasha stopped in mid-sentence as a blast of music rocked the hi-fi system. There was a peal of laughter from the boys as a group of girls entered the tent. 'Everyone's here!' Sasha jumped from Alissa's lap, clapping her hands. 'I'm going to find Bas. He's just gone to get Dr Darvill.'

Alissa watched her daughter with a mixture of protective pride and affection. Despite Mike's death, Sasha had grown into a bright and confident little girl. Alissa had vowed that nothing would threaten her happiness or stability of mind and she had tried to be both mother and father to her daughter.

It had been difficult at times with the pressure of home and career, but she hoped she'd achieved the best she could for Sasha. She was reluctant to say more to Sasha than was necessary regarding her relationship with Max. After today there would be more searching questions - questions even she didn't know the answer to.

Just then Max entered the tent and their eyes met briefly as he looked her way. Almost as if he'd known what she'd been thinking, he went down on his haunches and spoke to Sasha. Alissa watched them, noting the shy expression on her daughter's face and the eagerness with which she responded to him. How quickly her daughter would learn to love and trust - a terrifying thought if that love and trust were not given to the right person.

Alissa shivered. With a pang of sadness she shook her head a little, as if trying to clarify her thoughts. Tonight everyone seemed so happy and being here at Max's house seemed so natural that she really thought she must be worrying for nothing. Children were resilient, often more so than adults. She knew that from her work, as well as observing Sasha's own recovery from her father's death.

Just then Max pointed to the buffet table and Sasha nodded, sliding her hand into his as he rose and they walked towards it. Bas ran into the marquee and joined them and Max handed each child a plate, then left them to select their suppers.

What could she read in his expression as he turned and walked towards her? she wondered. Could it possibly reflect what was going on in her mind, too? He came and sat down, his long jean-clad legs outstretched as he made himself comfortable beside her. She felt so right in his company. How easy it was to imagine that they'd known each other for a lifetime. Despite all her attempts to remain objective about their affair, she couldn't help but feel the way she did.

By half past eight the patch of grass in the middle of the tent was crowded with gyrating teenagers. Sasha and Bas had exhausted themselves and had returned to the house to amuse themselves. Max leaned forward and touched her arm, raising his voice above the music. 'Shall we leave them to it and go inside as well?' he shouted.

Alissa nodded and, hand in hand, they made their way from the marquee and out into the warm evening air. Max slid his arm around her as they walked towards the house. 'Were we really as noisy as that when we were young?' he asked as she leaned against him.

She laughed. 'Probably more so.'

He grimaced. 'I suspect the generation gap is showing.'

'Not very much,' she teased him. 'I think we left before it became too obvious.'

He pulled her against him and whispered, 'Let's find a quiet corner somewhere and then we can behave as though we were also fifteen.'

She giggled. 'You'll have to refresh my memory. It was a long time ago.'

'My pleasure,' he growled, and his grey eyes glimmered with promise.

But no sooner had they reached the house than Bas and Sasha came running in from the front garden. 'Mummy's here!' Bas called breathlessly. 'She's brought Aaron his present. It's a new hi-fi system and it -'

Max stiffened as Priss walked through the door wearing a stunning pink suit. 'Max - darling,' she called as she approached, her slender figure, balanced on high heels, seeming to glide across the floor.

It was then that Alissa noticed the suitcase and accompanying set of hand luggage tucked by the open front door.

With a sinking sensation she realised that Priss's visit wasn't intended to be a fleeting one. Suddenly all Alissa's doubts crystallised as Priss leaned forward and kissed Max on the cheek.

'I wasn't expecting you today,' Max said sharply.

Priss looked from one to the other then smiled at Alissa. She was about to speak to Alissa when another figure appeared at the front door.

'Clare!' shouted Bas. 'Aaron thought you weren't coming!'

'I'm sorry I'm late,' Clare Fardon apologised in a small voice as she walked hesitantly towards them.

'Not at all,' Max said politely. 'You know Mrs Haigh.' He gestured to Priss who said nothing, her dislike of the girl clearly obvious. 'And this is Dr Leigh.'

Alissa smiled. 'Hello, Clare.'

The shock was evident on the teenager's face as she recognised Alissa. However, Max beckoned her at once, explaining that Aaron and his friends were outside in the marquee.

When they had gone Priss turned to Alissa, her eyes narrowing. 'It's good of you to offer to help Max in my absence,' she said coldly. 'However, now that I'm here it hardly seems necessary for you stay.'

Alissa stood in astonished silence, wondering if she heard correctly. Before she could ask Priss to repeat herself, the pink-suited figure had turned, lifted one of the smaller bags standing beside the front door and sedately ascended the stairs.

'Mummy, don't you feel very well?' Sasha was asking, sliding her fingers into Alissa's hand, tugging it sharply in order to gain her attention.'What ...?' Alissa looked down into her daughter's anxious face. She realised that Sasha had sensed the shock that seemed to fill every part of her as she tried to respond.

'Oh, no, I'm fine, darling. It's just a headache,' she managed shakily.

'Do you want a drink of water? I'll come with you if you like.'

Alissa nodded as Sasha grasped her hand tightly and they walked along to the kitchen. Alissa did her best to think sensibly and not panic. But how could she get through the rest of the evening now after what Priss had said?

'Is Bas's mummy coming back to live with Dr Darvill?' Sasha asked, as they entered the kitchen and Alissa opened a cupboard door and reached in for a glass.

'I don't know, sweetheart,' Alissa responded weakly.

'Bas's mummy is quite pretty,' Sasha said.

Alissa blinked hard and swallowed on the lump in her throat. She nodded. 'Yes, she is.'

'Not as pretty as you, though.' Sasha watched her mother, her anxious eyes taking in Alissa's distracted movements.

Placing the glass on the worktop, Alissa hugged Sasha against her. What dreadful mistake had she made in assuming - hoping - that Priss wasn't still in Max's life? Humiliated and angry, she squeezed her eyes tightly shut to prevent the tears of humiliation falling as Sasha curled against her.

A feeling of desperation was filling her. She only knew that she wanted to be as far away from this house as possible. The past suddenly poured back into her thoughts and became like a physical pain in her chest. Could it possibly be that she was the type of person who attracted men like Mike and Max - men that were always tied to women who wouldn't let them go?

The sounds of the music drifting in through the open window brought her back to the present and she straightened up, smiling at Sasha. At once Sasha yawned, rubbing her eyes and leaning against Alissa as she reached out to pour the water into the glass.

'Are you tired, darling?'

Sleepily Sasha nodded. 'A bit.'

'Then I think it's time to go. Run along and get your things. Say goodbye to Bas and I'll tell Dr Darvill we're leaving.'

Sasha made no objection and it was with a wave of relief that Alissa felt that she'd managed to hide her feelings and that it would seem to Sasha quite natural to be leaving at this hour.

As Alissa turned back to rinse her glass she couldn't help her reaction to the sight she saw from the kitchen window. In the dusk, two figures stood close together by the marquee, instantly recognisable.

Turning away sharply, she reached out to steady herself. She knew what she had to do. And she had to do it swiftly. A few minutes later Sasha was curling up to sleep on the back seat of the car. And Alissa was driving towards home.

CHAPTER 29

At some unearthly hour during the night, Alissa had accepted she wouldn't sleep. She'd made herself a cup of tea, while listening to the morning chorus, and finally watched dawn break.

The facts were plain enough, she decided as streaks of gold and scarlet spun across the sky. Priss had no intention of setting Max free. His inability to see that was obviously an indication of his affection for her and not, as he'd insisted, his concern for the boys.

Alissa fought back the tears. Eventually, in an attempt to compose herself, she dressed and made breakfast for Sasha. One thing was certain - she couldn't go on all day like this. Hurriedly she brushed the hot moisture from her eyes and pulled back her shoulders, determined not to let Sasha see her distress.

When Sasha came downstairs half an hour later, Alissa was wearing a bright smile and was packing the picnic hamper.

'Where are we going?' Sasha asked as she sat on a stool in the kitchen and surveyed the contents of the hamper.

'To the beach,' Alissa responded quickly. 'I've phoned Caroline Lewis and asked if Amy would like to come with us for the day.'

'Is your headache better this morning?' Sasha fiddled with the buttons of her pyjama top, frowning up at her.

'Much, thank you, darling.' Alissa tucked fruit and nuts into a plastic dish and placed it in the hamper. 'Now, when I've finished this, we'll find the beach things and take them out to the car.'

Sasha appeared to accept this and slipped down from the stool. 'Can I wear my new swimming costume?'

Alissa nodded. 'But bring a T-shirt. You'll need to cover up if it's very hot.'

Suddenly Sasha looked brighter. 'Amy's a good swimmer. Can we take the dinghy?'

Alissa brushed strands of hair from her daughter's eyes and nodded. 'If the waves aren't too rough we can play in the shallows.'

Sasha ran to the door. 'I'll get changed into my shorts,' she called over her shoulder, then stopped to turn back and look at Alissa, wrinkling her freckled nose. 'Bas won't be having half such good fun as us.' She giggled. 'His mummy will make him dress up and go out to a restaurant or something. And he'll have to sit there for hours, listening to grown-ups talking.'

Realising that Sasha and Bas must have discussed his mother's arrival, Alissa hoped Sasha hadn't linked their abrupt departure the previous night with Priss's appearance. However, she soon put this worry from her mind as Sasha ran up the stairs, singing.

CHAPTER 30

ASTRID ARRIVED BACK on Sunday evening from London where, as usual, she'd spent the weekend with friends. The beach had proved a perfect distraction and, with the two girls to occupy, Alissa soon realised that she had overcome the blues that had threatened at the start of the day.

She'd deliberately left the answering machine off, and as they didn't arrive home until late she didn't know whether to be relieved or disappointed at the dull red light which should have been flickering to denote a saved call.

On Monday morning she knew she had to face going into work. Dressing carefully in a new pale blue dress and high heels, washing her hair and conditioning it until it shone, she felt at least that her appearance gave no hint of the hurt and humiliation she'd felt on Saturday evening.

Ironically, she'd forgotten it was Max's day off this week. Here again, when she should have been relieved she was disturbed and restless. Her busy day passed quickly and that evening she went home too tired to spend time torturing herself with a mental repeat of Saturday's nightmare. The phone rang twice, but she didn't answer it, knowing it couldn't be the surgery as Erin was on call. If it was Max, she still didn't trust herself to speak to him.

The following day was more difficult. Max was in the surgery, leaning over the Reception desk as she walked in. Immediately her heart raced and her legs felt weak. He looked up and they glanced at one another, politely saying good morning.

Eager to reach her room, she didn't pause, grateful for once for the early morning rush of patients. At midday, when she had completed her list, there was a knock on her door and Max entered.

'Lyn said that you were free.' He came and stood in front of the desk, his face grave. 'I think we should talk, don't you?'

'There's nothing to discuss, Max. I think we both know that.'

'I don't understand your attitude.' He frowned, his eyes concerned. 'I've been trying to telephone you. Why are you avoiding my calls and why did you leave on Saturday night without talking to me first?'

'Wasn't it obvious?'

'I understand that Priss's appearance must have been a surprise, but not a reason for you to leave as you did.'

'Well, I certainly couldn't stay under those circumstances,' she said as her voice trembled. 'This is doing neither of us any good.' Alissa stood up, her cheeks burning. 'Max, there's obviously no point in us continuing to see one another.' She couldn't stay after what Priss told her, even though he didn't know this. It was evident that Priss must have planned to come to the party all along and she was now making it clear that Alissa's presence was unwanted. If Max wasn't aware of the fact that his ex-wife would never set him free, it could only be that he'd chosen to ignore the truth because he was still in love with her.

Alissa swallowed and lifted her chin, a wave of recollection going over her of the arguments she'd had with Mike. He'd always made her feel that she was in some way responsible for his affair with Fiona. He'd even persuaded her that he'd finished with Fiona, and she'd believed him for a while.

When she'd discovered they were still seeing one another there had been tears and bitter quarrels, but each time she'd forgiven him. Well, she'd never allow that situation to happen again.

She'd had Sasha to think of then, a daughter who'd needed and loved her father. Thank God, she would never have to reproach herself for having left Mike before his death. But now the circumstances were entirely different. And Saturday had shown her that there could never be a future for her and Max. She opened her mouth to speak, but the phone rang.

Max stood in silence as she answered it. For a few moments Alissa listened to Jean Jeffs, then very slowly, after having spoken a few words of condolence, replaced the receiver.

'Eamon Jeffs,' she said quietly as all thoughts of a personal nature emptied from her mind, 'died at half past nine this morning. Jean found him in his taxi in the garage. He used some rubber tubing to filter the exhaust into the cab.

By the time they got to him it was far too late ...'

For a while the suicide of Eamon Jeffs left everyone shocked and saddened. The circumstances of his death and the note he'd written to Jean on that early September morning left no doubt in the Coroner's mind that he'd taken his own life while the balance of his mind had been disturbed.

Often Alissa wondered if she could have done more to help him. As with all tragic events, there remained the feeling of failure. However, as he'd never been her patient and she'd only been linked to him by the fact he'd walked into the surgery after the accident, she was left wondering what more she could have done to help him.

Finally, after several attempts to call on Jean and finding her not at home, she learned from one of the girls on Reception, who lived in the same road as the Jeffs, that Jean had moved to Scotland. Very soon the house was put up for sale and Alissa was forced to accept the fact that the Jeffs' brief appearance in her life was now over.

Ironically, the news of the death of Eamon Jeffs had interrupted the discussion Alissa had been having with Max and, as though Fate had intervened again, it was never resumed. The days passed by and their paths crossed briefly. Discreetly she avoided Max, and he, too, seemed to be avoiding her.

The children returned to school for the autumn term and Alissa received small items of news by way of her daughter. From the way Bas was speaking of his mother, it seemed certain she was living at the house. On one occasion Sasha reported that she'd seen Priss delivering Bas to school. That was the final confirmation for Alissa, and she vowed to establish a framework of existence with Max, hoping that time would heal her aching heart and that life eventually might return to normal.

However, by mid-September it was clear this could not be achieved. Only addressing one another when necessary, they moved cautiously around the surgery, avoiding the staffroom where they might meet by chance. When Alissa left the surgery at night she waited until the Discovery was gone from the car park.

One crisp, bright, autumn morning she pulled up in the car park and opened her car door just as the Discovery drew up beside her Ford. Max looked tired as he closed the driver's door and turned to face her. It hurt to see his guarded expression and she found herself silently gazing at him, unable to speak the words that were lodged in her throat.

'I was hoping I'd see you,' he said quietly.

She swallowed, her fingers tightening around her case. 'Were you?' she asked weakly.

He nodded. 'Betty and Jamie are coming in this morning. They asked to see us both.'

She was bitterly disappointed. For one moment hope had flared when he'd said he wanted to see her and all the pain had disappeared. But, composing herself quickly, she nodded, praying that he hadn't guessed her true thoughts. 'Is it good news, do you think?' she asked.

He shrugged. 'I've no idea. They're booked in for the last appointment of the morning. Will you be free then?'

'Yes, I should be.'

His eyes went over her as they stood in silence. It was the most beautiful of September mornings. A soft mist lay over the trees and clung to the leaves. The smell of bonfires was in the air. Everything about the day was perfect - except the way she was feeling right now, her whole body aching to go to him and be taken into his arms. The memory of the times they'd shared, the feeling of his body lying against her during those stolen nights, overwhelmed her.

'Are you all right?' he asked in concern as she swayed slightly.

'I...I'm fine,' she lied quickly, jerking away, fearing his touch and what it would do to her if she allowed her emotions to rise to the surface.

Because she said nothing he pulled back and in silence, as if distanced by an unseen hand, they began to walk to the surgery. Once inside they parted and Alissa hurried to her room, closing the door behind her as warm perspiration broke out under her clothes, causing them to stick unpleasantly to her skin. She leaned back, her body going limp as she closed her eyes. From out of nowhere came a deep sob, a wave of emotion rising up in her and almost drowning her.

She dropped her case to the floor and covered her face with her hands as more sobs followed, draining her of all her energy and leaving her weak. It was no use, she couldn't go on like this. The strain was intolerable. People would notice soon. She didn't know what was happening to her. Every bone and muscle in her body ached for Max. Inside her was a deep well of loneliness and she laid her hand on her stomach, trying to soothe the pain.

She opened her eyes and sighed deeply. 'What am I going to do?' she whispered, her voice desolate.

And the answer, which had vaguely been taking shape in her mind over the past few weeks, brought hot tears to her eyes. She swallowed and moved back to her desk, sinking down on the chair.

She loved this place, she loved the people, she loved her work. But she didn't know if she could go on seeing Max every day and pretending that nothing had happened between them. The only answer was, as she very well knew, to make her future elsewhere.

CHAPTER 31

BETTY AND JAMIE and the children were crowded into Max's office. Donna and Mark were seated on the floor, Sam was asleep in a pushchair, baby James lay in Betty's arms and Emily stood between her father and mother.

Jamie spoke first, his face flushed slightly. 'We've sold the farm and we leave Hayford Minster in a week's time. We thought we should come in and say goodbye.' He glanced tentatively at his wife. 'I think we owe you an apology, don't we, Betty?'

Betty nodded, her pretty face looking older and missing the energy that had always characterised her spirit. 'Yes,' she sighed. 'I suppose we do.'

'The farm's been bought for development,' Jamie explained as Betty declined to say more. 'You'd have to be a fool not to see the way farming is going these days. There's no profit in it and the hours are very hard on us. With the baby arriving, Betty needs more help with the children.' He looked at his wife, then back to Max and Alissa. 'We've decided to accept a job in the north of England. It's a manor house needing a couple to look after the estate. We have a cottage and all our bills will be paid. It's not what we would have chosen but the environment will still be rural.'

There was silence in the room as Betty looked down at the baby. She was clearly upset. Whatever had gone on between the couple, Alissa knew that Betty's dream of farm life was now over.

Jamie ruffled Emily's hair. 'On a lighter note, with this new job, I'll have weekends off and I intend to see that Emily gets all the extra help she needs.'

Max looked at Emily. 'If it hadn't been for Emily's phone call to us that day, who knows what might have happened?'

Alissa noticed that Emily had clearly benefited from the situation. At Jamie's prompting she handed Alissa a slip of paper she'd been holding.

'That's her sums,' Jamie explained. 'She's doing them every night now. We're setting time aside for it, aren't we, Betty?'

Betty looked up and nodded. 'Yes,' she agreed with little enthusiasm.

'With the new job,' Jamie went on, 'the children can come into work with me on occasions.' The silence that followed conveyed more than words as Betty and Jamie glanced at one another with mutual expressions of resignation. As the children scrambled to their feet and Betty followed them out into the corridor, Jamie lingered with Emily.

'As you can see, we've decided to stay together,' he said quietly. 'I'll never make a fortune and Betty has to accept that Poplar Farm has gone for ever.' He shrugged his broad shoulders. 'But that's life, I suppose. We're still young. We can still make a go of things in the north.'

Max nodded. 'I'm sure you will, Jamie. Good luck.'

'Thanks.' Jamie added with a smile, 'For everything.'

Max closed the door after the family had gone and he stood for a moment, without saying anything. 'A happy ending?' he said at last, his voice filled with irony as he looked at Alissa.

'I hope so.' She glanced through the window towards the car park. Jamie lifted Sam from his pushchair and Betty climbed up into their Land Rover, the mud from the farm still spattered over its dark green paintwork.

Max arched an eyebrow. 'All that heartache for want of a little communication... simple enough, it would seem, to achieve but damned hard to do in reality, it appears.' He looked at Alissa intently and she read the message in his eyes. His gaze held hers until at last, unable to reply, she looked away. Swallowing on the lump that had formed in her throat, she opened the door and left.

CHAPTER 32

Erin carried the supper tray from the kitchen and into her small front room. She was on call that evening and had decided not to prepare a cooked meal, opting instead for the ease of salad and fruit.

She was listening to a CD she had bought recently - a little light jazz that had no connection to memories of Simon. Fortunately he hadn't enjoyed her taste in music and, settling down at the table beside the window, she tried to summon up an appetite.

The fainting spell she'd had at work recently had caused her to pay more attention to her lifestyle. It was too easy to miss a meal since she had no one to cook for now. Kate and Patti had returned to Ireland and her mother and father had left to visit a relative in Kent. She looked about her as she began to eat the simple supper. The flat, once adequate, seemed small and dull. She needed some colour in her life, she realised, and as soon as the cottage was sold she'd look for somewhere else.

Halfway through her supper the phone rang. The paging service informed her of a patient needing a visit and Erin rang the number. It was Hannah Brent's mother. The problem was a repetition of the rash and hay fever Hannah had suffered previously and, pushing aside her meal, Erin resigned herself to making a visit.

It took her less than five minutes to drive to the Brent's' house. Mrs Brent was waiting at the door and led Erin to Hannah, who lay on a sofa in one of the downstairs rooms. It was clear her rash was much worse and she was wheezing badly.

'All she was doing was eating her tea,' Mrs Brent complained as she wrung her hands and pushed back her untidy hair. 'Then all of a sudden... this again!'

Erin glanced at the plate on the small table and the crust of a sandwich. 'What filling was in the sandwich?' she asked.

'Oh, just peanut butter.' Mrs Brent shrugged.

'Can you remember if Hannah had the rash last time she ate peanuts?'

'Well, no... or, perhaps, yes...she might have.' Mrs Brent sounded confused.

Erin opened her case and took out a pack of syringes. Filling one with adrenaline, she injected Hannah and, brushing the hair from the little girl's flushed face, waited for the drug to take effect.

It did so within seconds and very soon Hannah was no longer struggling to breathe.

'What did you do?' Mrs Brent asked in amazement.

'I believe Hannah is allergic to peanuts.' Erin helped the eight-year-old to sit up, turning eventually to Mrs Brent. 'I gave her an injection of adrenalin. It's used in the treatment of anaphylaxis - a severe symptom of allergy.'

'But why has it suddenly started to happen?' Mrs Brent frowned.

'That, I can't tell you, I'm afraid. What we must do is to go back to square one again and take a look at her diet.'

Mrs Brent sank into a chair. 'I've never been so frightened in all my life.'

'Yes,' Erin agreed sympathetically. 'Anaphylactic shock is frightening to witness and I'm afraid great care will have to be taken with Hannah's diet. Peanut oil is a commonly used cooking ingredient, and eliminating all foods that cause an allergic reaction is the only remedy.'

By the time Erin got back to her flat later that evening, she'd satisfied herself that this time Mrs Brent had complied with her suggestions. The episode had frightened her to the extent she would now co-operate.

Erin sat down on the sofa and gazed at the remainder of her own meal. Here she was, telling her patients to consider their diets, when her own eating habits could certainly be improved!

She laid her head against the cushions, letting a soft sigh escape as her eyes came to rest on a crystal figure of Cupid standing on the shelf above the fireplace. The ornament was the solitary reminder of her wedding day and had it not been given to her by Alissa it would have been tucked away in a box and moved to the attic. Generously, Alissa had insisted she keep the gift. It was an offer that Erin had accepted, in part for Alissa's benefit for it was only a few days previously her friend had revealed that her relationship with Max was over.

What was more distressing was that Alissa had hinted that her future at the practice was now in doubt. Although no more had been said, Erin guessed that Priss had caused trouble yet again, trouble that rippled dangerously through everyone's lives.

Sighing once more and trying to put these thoughts from her mind, Erin rose and wandered over to the fireplace. Her hand went up to the pale blue envelope standing to the right of the figurine. She took out the letter and read it once more. Nick's few words of consolation had comforted her. Her thoughts strayed back to the day she'd spent with him in the New Forest when they'd talked at length about their hopes and dreams.

Had Nick's tangled relationship survived after he returned to Canada? she wondered. Erin slid the piece of thin blue paper back in the envelope and sighed. 'Call me if ever you need to talk,' he had written.

She was tempted, but the moment passed and she replaced the letter on the shelf. Walking to the window, she looked out, her gaze coming to rest on the silhouette of the Minster tower. Its strong shape had faded into the night and for a few seconds the memory of the evening she'd spent with Nick came back, bringing with it the feel of the tender kiss he'd brushed on her lips as he'd said goodbye.

CHAPTER 33

ONE FRIDAY MORNING in late September Alissa walked into the office and found Jane, the secretary, pinning a notice on the board.

'A slight change in rota,' Jane said as Alissa walked forward to read it, 'but you probably know already about Dr Darvill's holiday next week.'

Alissa frowned. 'No, I don't think so... ' Her voice tailed off as she saw a line drawn through Max's name and an unfamiliar name substituted above it. 'Who's Dr Bellamy?'

'Dr Darvill didn't tell you?' Jane looked at her curiously.

'No,' Alissa was forced to admit. 'I expect it escaped his mind.'

'Yes, possibly,' agreed Jane, though she continued to stare at Alissa. 'Well, Dr Bellamy is a friend of Dr Darvill's and is coming to locum for us next week. Dr Darvill is going away to Paris - with you know who, I think.'

For a moment Alissa held her breath, then slowly let it out again, aware that the secretary was watching her.

'Second honeymoon, I shouldn't wonder,' Jane went on, 'though I can't imagine what on earth he sees in the woman.' She bent down and picked up the stack of A4 folders that lay on the desk. Walking to the door, she raised her eyebrows. 'Let me know if you want any work done before this evening, will you. Dr Leigh?'

'What?' Alissa dragged her eyes from the notice.

'I'd like to get things clear for next week, just in case Dr Bellamy needs help with our computer software.'

'Oh, yes, all right, Jane.' When the door had closed Alissa turned toward the notice again, forcing herself to accept the words before her eyes. A second honeymoon, Jane had said.

Alissa felt her stomach turn over. She sank down onto the chair and tried to recover her breath. Max had deliberately avoided her over the past weeks and now she knew why. She didn't know how long she sat there, but by the time she found herself thinking clearly again she was back in her room and it was time to see her first patient.

What made things worse was Sasha's dismay when she returned from school on Monday. 'Bas has got a week off from school,' she told Alissa miserably. 'Our teacher told us that he's gone to Paris.'

Alissa was preparing the vegetables for supper. 'Oh, that's nice,' she answered quickly.

'No it's not,' Sasha declared, as she helped to arrange the lettuce in the salad bowl. 'He didn't tell me he was going.'

'Well, perhaps he didn't know,' Alissa offered reasonably.

Sasha came to stand by Alissa at the sink. 'Have you talked to Astrid yet?'

Surprised at the swift change of subject, Alissa frowned. 'What do you mean, darling?'

'She said last night she's going back to Sweden. She said she was going to tell you today.'

'Oh, I see.' Alissa turned to face her daughter. 'Well, it's been a busy day. I expect Astrid will talk to me when she comes home from her evening class.'

Sasha leaned her elbows on the worktop, tears just kept at bay. 'I don't want her to leave us.'

Alissa reached out and drew Sasha into her arms. 'Darling, we knew Astrid had to go back to Sweden some time, didn't we?'

Sasha was silent for a moment then mumbled, 'Why does everything have to change, Mummy? Why can't it always stay the same?'

It was a question Alissa found hard to answer considering what lay ahead. Before long there would be many more changes in her daughter's life. She hated to uproot Sasha from the happy life they'd established in Hayford Minster, but to go on working with Max under the prevailing circumstances was impossible.

She glanced over Sasha's head at the medical journal lying on the kitchen table. She'd made several phone calls during the weekend regarding the availability of practice partnerships, the results of which would arrive in the post over the next few days. But she would keep that to herself for the time being, until she found the right moment to break the news to Sasha.

The first week of October was damp and drizzly, with mists and rain that persisted over the trees and fields like a wet, grey blanket. During Max's absence Dr Bellamy, a retired doctor who had substituted as locum for Max at his previous practice, proved popular with the patients. resigned to the inevitable, Alissa began the process of distancing herself from her patients. On the whole it had been a good year, she rationalised. Eamon Jeffs's suicide and Erin's personal drama had affected everyone for a time, but there had been successes too. Betty and Jamie had patched up their differences and Esme Kelly and Orion had settled in Hayford Minster. But it wasn't until the last day of the week that Alissa was to discover what had happened to Clare Fardon.

As her afternoon surgery ended, Clare walked into her room and sat down, as she had the first time, dropping her schoolbag to the floor. This time, though, the teenager was smiling.

'I've come to thank you, Dr Leigh,' Clare said at once. That night at Aaron's party - you didn't let on that you knew me.'

Alissa smiled. 'No, I wouldn't have done that, Clare.'

'Even though you were friends with Aaron's dad?' Clare asked uncertainly.

'That doesn't make any difference,' Alissa assured her. 'Whatever is said between a doctor and his or her patient goes no farther than the consulting room, otherwise doctors would have very few patients.' She laughed and Clare laughed, too, but Alissa couldn't help but wonder what conclusions Clare had drawn regarding herself and Max.

'Anyway, I just wanted to say thank you,' Clare went on. 'Do you know that Aaron and I have split up?'

Alissa shook her head. 'I'm sorry to hear that.'

'We're still good friends,' Clare said reflectively. 'We decided we were too young to get into all that stuff I told you about.'

'You mean, the question of contraception?'

Clare looked embarrassed. 'My dad would have gone crazy if he'd found out I was on the Pill, not to mention Aaron's mum. She didn't like me anyway and, quite honestly, I didn't like her. It all got too heavy for us, what with one thing and another. It's better we go our separate ways until we're older.'

'I'm sure you and Aaron have made the right decision,' Alissa said, but didn't comment further. Clare glanced at her wristwatch and rose to her feet. 'I'd better go. I'm meeting Mum at the Minster and we're going to do some shopping. Bye, Dr Leigh, and thanks again.'

'Goodbye Clare.' Alissa stood up and accompanied the girl to the door, aware that the teenager was eager to be on her way. 'I'm glad everything worked out well in the end.'

'Me, too.' Clare smiled and Alissa watched her disappear down the corridor. She walked back into her room, trying to dismiss the unsettling feeling that Clare's appearance had triggered. It seemed that time had resolved Clare's problems, but in her own case a week without Max's presence at the surgery had only served to remind her how much she missed seeing him.

Each time she thought of the future the vacuum grew inside her. It was only by reminding herself that she had Sasha's happiness to think of that she was able to remain objective.

Alissa turned back to her computer and logged off.

It was time to go home.

By Sunday evening Alissa had scrutinised the details of two West Country practices which had replied to her enquiries. She knew the details almost by heart, had studied the beautiful coloured prints of the Truro surgery. The second practice, at Dartmouth, had sent her pictures by email, which she had printed out on the computer, and they now stood propped against a book on her desk.

Both practices had invited Alissa to visit, which she fully intended to do the following week. The decision, once taken, had been surprisingly simple to put into action. She was due for several days' leave and she'd telephoned Kirstie this morning to confirm them. She would ring Sasha's headmistress in the morning and explain that Sasha would be away from school for two days. Even Astrid's departure in November would coincide with her own.

All that remained was the selling of Green Gables, though she foresaw no problem with this. The house would be put into the hands of an agent, the keys handed over as they moved out.

Alissa sighed, stretched her back and rotated her head. She was seated in her study and the house was quiet. Sasha was fast asleep and Astrid at the cinema with a friend. All she had to do now was finish this letter and confirm a time...

Suddenly a knock at the front door made her jump. Thinking it must be Astrid returning early, she smoothed down her skirt and went to answer it. When she opened the door she stood for a moment, unable to believe who she was seeing.

The tall, broad-shouldered figure illuminated under the porch light moved towards her. Silver-grey eyes glittered as they studied her. Dressed in jeans and a dark blue sweatshirt, Max narrowed his eyes against the light. 'Are you busy?' he asked, his voice low as his eyes went past her and into the hall beyond.

'I - ' she began, then stopped as he frowned.

'You've company?'

'No, but - '

'I knocked because I didn't want to wake Sasha,' he said before she could continue. 'I take it she's asleep?'

'Yes,' she heard herself saying in a strained voice. 'She's asleep.' She swallowed and finally stepped back. 'Come in.'

He entered and she inhaled his scent, blown in with him on the crisp night air. She closed the door, playing for time, trying to think what he could want and why he was here. When she turned to face him she said simply, 'You'd better come into the study. I've been working in there and it's warm.'

He nodded and she led the way, her heart thudding as she gestured to a chair beside her desk. Almost at once his eyes fell on the photographs and he stopped abruptly, his face draining of colour.

'So it's true, then,' he said. 'You're leaving?'

She was shocked that he knew and for a moment she felt her face go ashen, but then she recovered herself and went to the easy chair and sat down, folding her hands in her lap, hoping it wasn't evident they were shaking. She looked up at him. 'Are you going to sit down?'

His eyes looked dark, haunted. 'Are you going to tell me why you're leaving?'

She lifted her chin as he lowered himself into the chair opposite her. 'Isn't it obvious?'

'No, it isn't. I'm afraid I've understood very little since the night of Aaron's party, only that after Priss's arrival you walked out. I realise it must have been a shock for you, but it was just as much of a surprise for me. I had no idea she would turn up.'

'Do you mind telling me who told you I was leaving?' she asked, finding it almost impossible to believe what he was saying. After all, he'd just spent a week away with Priss, she'd been living at the house -

'It was Erin,' he said quietly, breaking into her thoughts.

'I spoke to her a short while ago on the telephone. She said it was important I talk to you,' he added, his eyes locking with hers and holding them. 'She was reluctant to tell me more but from what she inferred I couldn't help but assume you were making plans to leave.' He glanced at the photographs. 'Just tell me why, Alissa.'

She paused, biting down on her lip. 'If you don't know, Max, I don't think I can tell you.'

He stared at her, shaking his head slowly, his eyes seeming to bore into her soul. 'All I can say is that I haven't slept for weeks, not since the night of the party. And when I sleep I dream of you, only to wake and find - ' He stopped, his eyes dark and troubled. 'Alissa, don't you realise you've shut me out of your life and there's no way I can get back in? You might as well be a million miles away, on some other planet. When I try to talk to you, you simply won't listen to reason.'

She couldn't believe what he'd just said. She swallowed again, and when at last she spoke the words came tumbling out in a rush, her heart pounding under her ribs as she spoke them. 'Do you seriously expect me to believe you when for the past weeks you've been living with Priss and have only just returned from your trip to Paris with her?'

'Paris?' He stood up, pushing back the chair, his body stiffening as he gazed down on her with incredulous eyes. 'What are you talking about?'

'I'm talking about your week away with Priss,' she said shakily, determined not to look away from his gaze, his eyes narrowing as he stared at her.

He shook his head slowly, his voice low. 'You're mistaken, Alissa, if you think Priss has been living at the house. And as far as Paris goes, I haven't been there in years.'

Alissa stared at him, her lips trembling. 'But...but I was told you were in Paris. One of the girls at work...they said - '

'Whoever it was, they gave you the wrong information,' he interrupted her quietly. 'Priss went to Paris with the boys and I travelled to Scotland to stay with friends.'

'You were in Scotland?' All she could do was stand there and try to absorb what he was telling her.

'I was asked to be godfather to a friend's son. It happened to coincide with the boys' week away, a trip arranged on the night of Aaron's party. Since Priss has no plans to return to England before the baby arrives, I was eager for them to spend some time with their mother.'

'The baby?' Alissa repeated bewilderedly. 'I...I don't understand.'

'Priss is expecting. The baby is due in February.' A smile touched his lips. 'Are you surprised?'

She nodded, swallowing. 'I...I thought that you and she, that you and Priss were...'

Max crooked an eyebrow. 'Priss married Claude a few days before

Aaron's birthday, hence the flying visit. They wanted to make the baby's birth legitimate. I'm relieved to say that Priss still retains some old-fashioned values, though it might not be evident in very much else that she does.'

'You mean she was already married on the night of Aaron's party?'

He nodded, his eyes going over her face, but this time an expression of amusement was in them. 'If you'd waited a few minutes longer that Saturday night you'd have met Claude. They were staying at a hotel in town for a few days and Priss had told him that she wanted to break the news to me alone. God knows why. For the maximum dramatic effect, no doubt, knowing Priss.' He shrugged, taking a breath before adding, 'I refused to allow her to tell the boys until the party was over. It was Aaron's night and I intended it to remain that way.'

'You mean Priss didn't stay at the house that night?' she blurted.

He looked astonished. 'Of course she didn't. Whatever gave you that idea?'

'Well, Priss did,' Alissa responded uncertainly, her cheeks flushed as she explained what had been said. 'And then one of the girls at work told me that you'd taken her to Paris,' she ended in a rush. 'Naturally, I put it all together and - '

'If you'd waited and let me explain,' he interrupted gently, a hint of reproach in his tone, 'then it would have been obvious what Priss was up to. And don't you know by now that the grapevine thrives on gossip? Priss has always managed to meet her critics' highest expectations. I'm afraid she probably always will.' A smile parted his lips as he reached out to draw her into his arms. 'Whatever has been going on in that head of yours, my darling?'

Shaking her head wordlessly, she realised the terrible mistake she'd made on that night, believing all Priss had said and done to deliberately mislead her. She stood there for some seconds, her mouth opening, but the words wouldn't come. Tears filled her eyes and before she could think what was happening his warm lips came down on hers, his fingers brushing back the hair from her hot cheeks.

'Don't cry, my sweet.' He gazed into her eyes, smoothing the dampness away with the pads of his thumbs. 'Priss and I were over years ago,' he told her quietly. 'I've tolerated her presence in my life only for the boys' sake, but I couldn't seem to make you see that.' His voice was soft and husky as he added, 'Oh, Alissa, don't you know how much you mean to me? Since I met you everything has changed.'

Her voice was barely a whisper. 'I didn't know you felt that way. I thought...I thought so many things...'

'Me, too,' he murmured as she stared up at him. 'I didn't know how you felt. About me, about the boys, about a life together. What could I offer you? A ready-made family and all the problems that I seemed to be having.'

'Max, I love the boys. And I - ' She met his gaze. 'I...I love you.'

'Oh, God, Alissa, you don't know what it means to me to hear you say that.' He looked at her for a long while, then sighed. 'That night, in the garden, when I told Priss I was in love with you - '

'That's what you were telling her - that you loved me?' 'A wrong moment if ever there was one,' he acknowledged ruefully. 'Priss has never liked letting go of anything that was once hers. You saw how she was with young Clare Fardon. She hated to think she was losing Aaron.' Alissa sighed, wondering how she could have possibly been so gullible. 'She went into your bedroom, Max. She was so convincing.'

'But didn't you realise what she was up to?'

Alissa shook her head, feeling guilty and miserable. 'I took it that she'd come back to live at the house. Even Sasha said that she saw Priss driving Bas to school.'

'That was true.' Max nodded. 'But it was only for a few days while his mother and Claude were staying in Hayford Minster.'

'Oh, Max, you can't imagine what's been going through my mind,' she breathed, feeling light-headed with relief.

He shook his dark head. 'I should have guessed what was happening.' His voice was soft now, his gaze melting over her. 'I intended to propose to you on the night of Aaron's party when everyone had gone. I was left alone to wonder what in heaven's name had happened.' He sighed, a shudder going through his body and passing into hers. 'Oh, my darling, what fools we've been.'

She looked up at him, her heart bursting with a happiness she felt she didn't deserve. She'd mistaken Max for Mike, had looked for the same character traits and flaws which had haunted her for so many years. She'd allowed other people to influence her when she should have believed in him.

'So...' he whispered, lifting her chin towards him and gazing into her eyes. 'What are you going to do about all that correspondence lying on your desk?'

She smiled, her fingers running up into the thick softness of his hair, feeling the warmth of his skin and the strong arch of his neck. 'I'm going to leave it all until the morning.'

'And what, may I ask, are you going to do about it then?'

'What do you suggest I do?' she asked softly.

'Write back and say that you've changed your mind...' He bent down to press his lips over hers, his tongue teasing her mouth with soft, tender kisses. 'Because now you have the best excuse in the world - one nobody could argue with.'

She closed her eyes as he ran his hands over her shoulders and arms until they rested on the soft curve of her waist, pulling her firmly against him until an audible sigh escaped her lips. 'I do?' she breathed expectantly.

'Of course. You have a wedding to arrange,' he murmured, 'a wedding we are just about to confirm - providing the bride-to-be says yes.'

When she opened her eyes he was smiling at her. The expression on his face made it clear that he wouldn't set her free from his arms until she'd given him her assent.

And even then, she realised joyfully, it might take all night long to give...

ENJOYED THIS BOOK?

You can make a big difference to the success of Dishy Doc by leaving a review with Amazon. I value your comments enormously and will always work hard toward making Dishy Doc Series as entertaining as I can. A single word or one line review will help the books on their way. Thank you!

If you would like to receive Parker Dee's news and updates on all her romance series, please sign up for her newsletter
  http://www.carolrivers.com/subscribe-romance.html

ABOUT THE AUTHOR

Carol's family comes from the historic Isle of Dogs, East London, UK. She's drawn from this fascinating background to create her gritty dockland novels and is a Sunday Times bestselling author for Simon & Schuster. A lifelong fan of medical dramas like ER and Grey's Anatomy, she has now launched her contemporary series of Dishy Doc medi-roms, published through Amazon's KDP.

Carol loves to hear from readers and can always be found on FB, Twitter and Google+.

She would especially like to thank all the Amazon reviewers who have purchased and reviewed her novels. She takes great heart and inspiration from the comments. Why not visit her webpages.

http://www.carolrivers.com/romance.html

And sign up for her newsletter

http://www.carolrivers.com/romance.html
www.carolrivers.com
carolrivers@sky.com

ALSO BY PARKER DEE / CAROL RIVERS

Dishy Doc Series

English Nurse, Playboy Doctor

Book One

Return of Doctor Deceiver

Book Two

Doctor Don't Leave

Book Three

Doctor Please Stay

Book Four

Love in the Practice

Book Five

<u>Italian Doctors</u>

Italian Doctor, Single Mum

Book One

Italian Doctor, Pregnant Partner

Book Two

Also by Carol Rivers

East End Romance Sagas

Gritty historical family dramas set in the East End of London

Seasonal Christmas themed books

CHRISTMAS TO COME

TOGETHER FOR CHRISTMAS

A WARTIME CHRISTMAS

IN THE BLEAK MIDWINTER

Best selling Lizzie Flowers series

LIZZIE OF LANGLEY STREET

THE FIGHT FOR LIZZIE FLOWERS

Page-turning wartime books

EAST END ANGEL

TOGETHER FOR CHRISTMAS

A WARTIME CHRISTMAS

Gritty East End family dramas

A PROMISE BETWEEN FRIENDS

A SISTER'S SHAME

EAST END JUBILEE

COCKNEY ORPHAN

LILY OF LOVE LANE

EVE OF THE ISLE

BELLA OF BOW STREET

2017

MOLLY'S CHRISTMAS ORPHANS

LILY'S CHRISTMAS WORKHOUSE BABY AND BONNY'S CHRISTMAS ANGEL (short stories)

KATE'S EAST END CARUSO (short story)

Copyright © Carol Rivers 2017

All Rights Reserved

No part of this novel may be used or reproduced in any manner whatsoever without written permission from the author. This is a work of fiction. Names, characters, places and incidents are products of the author's imagination. Any resemblance to actual events, locations, organisations or persons, living or dead, is entirely coincidental.

Printed in Great Britain
by Amazon